Fire Hides
Everywhere

Fire Hides Everywhere

Julian Feeld

Winchester, UK
Washington, USA

First published by Zero Books, 2017
Zero Books is an imprint of John Hunt Publishing Ltd., Laurel House, Station Approach,
Alresford, Hants, SO24 9JH, UK
office1@jhpbooks.net
www.johnhuntpublishing.com
www.zero-books.net

For distributor details and how to order please visit the 'Ordering' section on our website.

Text copyright: Julian Feeld 2016

ISBN: 978 1 78535 549 3
978 1 78535 550 9 (ebook)
Library of Congress Control Number: 2016954750

A CIP catalogue record for this book is available from the British Library.

Design: Stuart Davies

Printed and bound by CPI Group (UK) Ltd, Croydon, CR0 4YY, UK

We operate a distinctive and ethical publishing philosophy in all
areas of our business, from our global network of authors to
production and worldwide distribution.

Acknowledgments

There are many people to whom I owe much. I'd like to thank Remi Slade-Caffarel, Genevieve Gagne-Hawes, Mathilde Huron, Kathleen Craig, Louisa Pillot, and Alicia Heimersson for reading, being read to, editing, and generally providing help along the way. I'd also like to thank my family for their love and support: Audrey, Gerard, Christian, Claire... that's you. In this third and perfectly acceptable sentence I think I will direct the stream of my gratitude towards Alfie Bown for his generous disposition and help in getting *Fire Hides Everywhere* into the hands of the Zero Books team, whom I'd also like to thank for their support and expertise, particularly Emma Jacobs for the copy-edit. Finally, a little word for you, dear reader: thank you. For picking this novel up. For reading literary fiction in general. And for accepting to come on this journey with me.

1.

The twins had blonde hair and dull green eyes and tanned skin. Sabine, whose hair was longer than Marc's, wore a thick scar near her pubis where Christophe had removed her appendix. The old man had forced the child supine atop the dinner table and bound her there with old rags. He had unseamed her bloated flesh with a match-singed razor blade and removed the mucilaginous growth with his bare hands as the other children watched from outside the farmhouse. Their eyeballs were locked, faces warped in a spill, down into the whitewashed wood of the window frame, where the glass pooled thick and hazy. There a horsefly beat continually against the thin upper-pane, falling to the sill below, wings an opalescent blue.

Sabine screamed like a stuck pig until Christophe soaked a rag in chloroform and pressed her to sleep. He worked slowly and precisely, gaze rising to meet Marc's periodically, baring his teeth to discourage the boy from shattering the window with a rock.

Afterwards Christophe sewed the gash with copper wire to prevent Sabine from tearing the stitches apart. He filed her nails until they were dull and useless, but in the weeks to come Sabine worked at the wound with small twigs and rocks until it turned a reddish purple and filled with pus. Finally he rode his bicycle along the main road, set upon by ruined colza and wheat fields, scattered farmhouses, most destroyed, expanses of oak, hornbeam, and into Vailly, where he waded through crushed pillboxes in the backroom of a flooded pharmacy to find something that might save the child. Sabine did survive, but the scar remained, tumescent and pink, a crudely etched cave painting upon her flesh.

2.

Florian's hair was long and black and dry as burned straw, broken teeth protruding from lips dewy and larviform, above which a thin black moss gathered around a single beauty mark. The child was of bone and lopsided sinew, moving mostly on hands and feet, but standing now in the reeds at the edge of the pond where he sounded the surface for the secret shapes of fish beneath, skitting water spiders, undule of vertebrae in the muddy waters. He heard the old man's voice from the farmhouse.

We eat.

And licked his lips, smiled crooked, scratching the tip of his prick to feel the shivers. Abandoning the water he drew his feet through the grass until the mud fell away from them, and having passed the peach tree he raised his eyes to reorient himself, white ears atwitch. In the building across the courtyard, behind one of the grain silos, he crouched in the penumbra to clothe himself, the jumpsuit stiff and alien to his skin. Rats often whispered here in the half-dark behind the silos, but the old man's food was warm in his belly, and it was worth the discomfort.

3.

Christophe was tall and thin with a narrow face and small hard eyes, grey and lifeless. His skin was hard too, muscles flat grey rocks shifting about his thin frame as he placed bowls and spoons on the table. Beneath his bare feet, varicose, the terracotta shone a faded orange in the waning sunlight, steam rising to form droplets on the dark wood of the beams above. Christophe removed the soup from the fire and stirred it with a ladle. The smell of coriander.

Little ones sat huddled in a row at the end of the bench and looked slantwise at Lea. Her plump features, ruddy and curious, eyes golden brown. She worked her fingers into the crevices of the kitchen table where the grime had clotted and blackened. Little wormlets of crud curled away beneath her nails and they tasted sour and putrid. She let her tongue hang from her mouth and shook her head until they flung loose. Muffled laughter from the little ones. Lea looked at them and smiled, poking the one beside her in the ribs.

Marc and Sabine arrived together and sat on the bench opposite the others. She seemed lost with her drooping eyes, sunken, and Marc wore a fierce expression, sitting upright with his hand on her knee. Soon Florian entered the farmhouse and took a seat next to Sabine where he hunched over his bowl and watched his faint reflection in the porcelain as if it were something else altogether, something alive in its own right. Christophe ladled soup into each of their bowls and none of the children touched their spoons. Even Florian and the little ones knew to wait until Christophe had said the words.

The poor will eat. They will be satiated. Those who seek him will praise the lord. Let us pray to the lord who gives us this bread

Christophe paused for a very long time. He remained with his

3

long dry hands pressed together and his eyes closed. The children looked at each other and at Christophe, except Florian who looked at his soup. Lea's eyes were wet and full of worry.

Each day. Our father

Again there was a long pause and Lea's bottom lip began to tremble. A slow vinegar was spreading in the bottom of her stomach.

Our father

Christophe's eyelids were purple and thin. Lea thought she could see his eyeballs through the skin, waiting to see if she would pick up the spoon. Finally Christophe finished the prayer.

Our father protect us, lord god, and provide our weakness what it needs to survive. In the name of jesus christ our lord. Amen.

Christophe separated his hands and set his wrists against the table's edge. He opened his eyes and his mouth widened and his lips thinned and curved at the edges. Christophe's eyes remained inscrutable and he didn't blink. The children made noises as they ate their soup and Christophe watched them.

The vinegar had dissipated but Lea could feel it forming a sour headache. The soup took its warm course down her chest and into her belly. She felt like a river split in two. As she sipped from her spoon she noticed Marc's fingers. They were growing longer and thicker by the day, and beneath his nails what looked like dried blood. She turned to watch Christophe. He was staring at the wall, lip lopsided, the left side of his face unrecognizable to Lea.

Christophe knew the children were little fucking liars, each and every one of them. He knew to keep that in mind. To stay organized and make sure everything...

But during the prayer something had happened and he understood that too. There was no confusion in Christophe's mind. He needed to stay focused on what was important. No matter what, these children needed some form of structure, some form of instruction despite the steel-bound fact that he couldn't move his left wrist for several minutes. Then he could feel the sweat around his hand but not the flesh within. Then and little by little he regained feeling in his entire left side until he felt confident enough to attempt movement. Everything was the same as it always had been. Florian's bowl was shifted slightly forward because of the way he tended to lean into it. Otherwise all the bowls were equidistant and set correctly on the table. Even the soup tasted good. But Christophe wasn't an idiot. He knew exactly what had happened and also that it wouldn't get better over time.

Once they were finished eating, he waved the children from the table. As she walked away Lea looked over her shoulder but couldn't bring herself to look Christophe in the eyes. Anyways he was staring at his hand. The old man held the wrist and felt the bone beneath the skin. He ran his fingers along the top of his hand. Christophe straightened his arm and lifted it until it was level with his shoulder. He let it drop to his side.

He washed the bowls more slowly than usual and used a rag to dry each of them carefully. When everything was in its place once more, he walked over to the sofa and sat quietly with his eyes closed and thought about the children and imagined himself beneath the cold hard dirt of the courtyard, stiff and dead and useless to them.

Lea's dream

I lie on the orphanage bed, adults visiting in groups of two, often a man and woman whispering, to weigh my immobile body and decide whether they'll select me as their own. I don't make noises and don't suck my fingers or scratch at the floor, but through my closed eyelids the usual disgust appears around their mouths, and before long they place their flowers at the foot of my bed, say a quick prayer, and walk on.

When you remove all things there's nothing but rain and silence. When they removed all things, the world still remained.

In my book of letters I see A for apples burned beneath the rain. I see B for bodies burned beneath the rain. I see C for cars burned beneath the rain. I see D for dinosaurs burned beneath the rain. I see E for elephants burned beneath the rain. I see F for Florian burned beneath the rain.

Books are lies, they show the colors of things that have disappeared. What exists now? Christophe exists now, and the farmhouse, and Florian exists, not burned by any fire.

4.

The marks left by the tractor wheels were full of stagnant water after the rains and they shone in diagonal stripes beneath the new sun. Florian stared at these strange snakes uncoiled and melted in a line. He thrust his stick into a puddle and the brown water swallowed his fingers and wrist and part of his forearm, then stopped. Florian ran his tongue over his sharp teeth. That's how far it reached, the water, down into the place that rarely spoke to him except in rumbles.

He forced himself to remember this particular water. There was a line of ants marching from the puddle to the grass, brown mud smeared all around the treadmarks, blades of grass like combed wet hair, dried stiff and thrown away from the trail.

Flies drank from the water and some of them crawled around Florian's eyes. He left them to their business. Flies didn't learn any lessons because they existed in several places at once. Waters were different because one of them was going to be the right one. It would have no mud at the bottom and he would let himself fall forwards into the place he sometimes saw when he closed his eyes, the place of shines where Florian knew he belonged. He knew this because of what happened when he slept, the way his body opened up and became larger than the largest of things and smaller than the smallest of things, in both directions and turning roughly from itself.

He crawled to the next puddle, crushing several ants beneath his knees. They stayed pressed into his flesh, disassembled and bloody. Around him the sun, the trees, the brambled fence with its barbed wire.

Lea liked to watch many things but especially Florian. She always felt very relaxed when she watched the boy, and her toes were soft and warm and her thighs were warm and her breasts numb and her belly ceased its noises. Even her mind stopped making the long humming sounds that broke in and out of words.

She watched from the bushes as Florian squatted over the puddle with his little prick hanging between his legs, spine stretching the skin of his back. Her face shone round and curious, small body of clay folded over itself.

When the boy had moved far enough down the path, Lea's blood now running in cooler pulses, she emerged from the foliage to study the tangle of grass behind the barbed wire, through which she had glimpsed some unusual color.

With much effort she pulled the bicycle loose from the brambles and through the barbed wire. Its yellow paint had chipped away, revealing a layer of speckled rust. A long bloody gash had formed on her forearm, but Lea did not notice. She swung a leg over the cross bar and felt the seat ooze lukewarm water through its cracked vinyl shell. She pushed the bicycle over and stood pinching at her wet underwear and making noises, eyes rolling wildly in their sockets. Lea hiked her dress and tucked the hem of it under her chin, removing her underwear and laying them carefully between two barbs on the wire.

She stood there for a moment, features molten, feeling the wind between her spread legs. Her eyes lifted and they looked out over the undulant weeds at the small clumps of trees in the distance. The dress slipped from beneath her chin and its hem fell back around her knees. She returned to the bicycle.

Lea pushed it up and held it steady, pressed the seat until the water ran out, stood astride the crossbar with both feet grounded, remembering how Christophe had pushed the pedals, how the wheels had turned, and so resolving that she would hop backwards onto the seat and push down in the same manner.

After the fall Lea clutched her leg and made noises, disturbing two blackbirds perched in the branches above. They cawed and spread their wings, took flight. The crossbar had smashed into Lea's shin and the pain travelled along the bone in lances. She bit her lip and hissed through her teeth, body tense and folded. The pain stayed a long time before receding, tears running down Lea's cheeks.

When finally she rose, the child was ready for her second fall. Even though she bruised her shoulder and split her knee Lea did not cry and barely made any noise at all.

She rode the bicycle along the dirt path until she crossed the departementale and found herself on the cracked asphalt road leading back to the farmhouse. The wheels of the bicycle spun easy now, dress pressed to Lea's body, hair lashing in her wake. Soon there was nothing but the dull roar of wind in the girl's ears.

Lea turned right onto the dirt path that sloped down towards the farmhouse. She could see the pond with its tiny island, the cement building with its abandoned grain vats, the dusty courtyard, its single tree.

The tires pushed small rocks out of the way, bouncing Lea along like a puppet. Her eyes were frozen wide and her mouth formed an unbroken croak as the bicycle rolled past the center of the courtyard. Behind her now the young sapling and it's soft grass. A large rock stood in her path. There came a split-second of absolute calm before the child hit the ground.

Christophe saw the whole thing. He had been sitting in the wooden rocking chair when the sound of the bicycle drew his attention. He rose from the chair, put down his book, and walked to the window. The old man's expression remained blank until Lea's body hit the ground. Only his lips tightened slightly.

Lea's body lay face-down and limp in the twisting dust. The old man made his way across the sunlit courtyard, bare feet bruising on the rocks. He placed one arm beneath the child's thighs and the other beneath her chest and transported Lea over to the grass where he rolled her onto her back, careful to support her neck and head as he lay her down. Lea's eyes were closed and her body disarticulated.

Merde.

But Lea had only been winded by the fall and soon she drew a long ragged breath. The old man stood above her with his arms at his side. His knees bent slightly as he hesitated. He looked at the farmhouse. Then he looked at the child.

You don't move. I will return.

The pain existed in many places at once and Lea didn't bother reaching for it. She lay on her back in the grass and wept, sky hard and blue with a single cloud etched there like a lonely wound. Christophe had promised to return, and Christophe never lied, not once, but for the moment she felt nothing but the cold thirst of the soil beneath her.

5.

Florian had found nothing. He made his way back up the path, heart pushing sullen blood, mind hot and scrambled. The itch was worsening and he bloodied his nails on his scalp. The shade of the tree up ahead, a place to lay and rest in the dark, in front of which Florian saw Lea's underwear caught on the barbed wire and waving in the wind like a piece of torn fur. He lifted them from the wire and pressed them to his nose. They smelled of Lea and she appeared, smiling through her stubby teeth, one of them missing, and wearing her usual blue dress.

In the boy's fist a balled-up piece of cloth with the imprint of the girl's excreta, some fragment of her becoming, a prize above all others. Lying in the shade beneath the trunk of the sprawling elm, Florian closed his eyes and rested until a warm blackness came over him. His fist remained rigid but Florian's heart was soft and brimming with wordless knowledge. The sounds of the forest fed his dreams with wild colors and shapes, and his seeking ceased.

6.

Christophe reemerged from the farmhouse carrying a black plastic box with orange latches. From it he produced a pair of scissors, kneeled over the child, and set to work. He cut the dress from hem to neckline, split the sleeves, and peeled it open. At first glance there were no serious wounds or broken bones. He removed sharp pebbles from her hip, chin, and palms. From these wounds seeped a watery blood. Christophe rinsed and dried them with a rag. Lea gritted her teeth.

Tell me if it hurts a lot.

He bent each of her joints and Lea clenched her jaw but did not complain. The girl had no broken bones. She had fallen loosely and many parts of her body had struck the ground at once. She was badly bruised and nothing more. Christophe dabbed at the new blood with a piece of cotton and applied bandages to the wounds. He lifted Lea gently from the grass and pulled the torn dress from beneath her body.

The old armoire hadn't been touched in at least a year and it creaked and moaned as he unlocked and opened it. On the second level and gathering dust he found the folded white dress where he had left it.

The child had gathered her knees to her chest and she was sitting below the sapling when Christophe returned. Marc stood above her with his hands in his pockets, Sabine not far behind him. She murmured something to her brother and they turned to watch the old man approach. He waved them away.

Begone.

The children retreated to the dusty periphery and watched. Christophe gestured for Lea to rise. She looked at him and looked at Marc. The old man hissed at the siblings and they turned to leave. Lea watched them walk towards the pond.

The old man helped Lea to her feet and she lifted her arms.

Once she was clothed Christophe walked over to the bicycle and inspected it. Lea clenched her fists and looked closely at the old man for signs of what might come next. She wanted to stay quiet but the word came anyway.

Mine.

Christophe held the bicycle and looked at Lea. She dared not approach him. Her body trembled and she stood with her bandaged palms open, fingers twitching. Christophe rolled the bicycle over to her and made her grip the handlebar. He let go of the bicycle and returned to the farmhouse. Lea was confused. She blinked and looked down at the bike and up at the farmhouse. Soon Christophe returned with a pump and a can of oil. He pumped the tires and oiled the gears. The old man lowered himself and listened to the tires. Satisfied, he stood again and spun the wheels. There were no leaks and they spun smoothly enough. He showed her how to use the breaks.

Do you understand?

She nodded. Through her tears Lea watched the old man gather all the nice things he had done for her and disappear into the farmhouse. She left her bicycle in the dirt and ran up to the window to look inside. Christophe was sitting in the rocking chair again, reading a book. He looked like a statue, bust unmoving. Only his eyes skipped back and forth on the page.

From behind Lea came the sound of footsteps in the dirt. She spun to see Marc with his cold eyes locked on her bicycle and his sister staring in that awful way. Lea hardened her face and walked past them as best she could, limping on her bruised hip. They stood and stared at her. Lea got on the bicycle and pedaled off, nearly falling again from the pain. She would have to hide the bicycle well. It belonged to her and so did the dress. She had paid for them both.

7.

The colza field was a blinding yellow, unharvested for genera-
tions and growing increasingly wild. On its northernmost edge,
among the remnants of a primitive forest, two children were busy
repairing their home. Sunlight made its way through the canopy
and fat brown slugs pulled along the white husks of fallen
birches. Weakened by rain and hollowed by rot, the dead
branches collapsed easily beneath Marc's feet. He grunted with
each kick and stood aside to let Sabine gather the splintered
wood. She flung these wet piles away from the cabanne until no
weakness was left in the structure and the siblings stood side by
side and stared at their handiwork. It was a crude and misshapen
home with a tent-shaped roof covered by clumps of turquoise
moss.

The scent of necrotic wood excited Sabine, the way it mingled
with her brother's sweat and formed a sharp, sweet odor that
wafted over the fossilized memories of their mutual past.
Sometimes she and Marc would undress and lie against each
other on the floor of the cabanne and in those moments Marc
could feel what remained very plainly. He would close his eyes
and picture their aches like two small fires built together in a
dark forest. When one of them threatened to extinguish, a flame
from the other would jump through the darkness to keep it
alight.

Marc scoured their surroundings for new branches to fill the
gaps. These he fastened to the structure with soiled lengths of
fishing line. Every so often he turned to look at Sabine, who
sought fresh patches of moss with which to repair the roof. He
watched as she thrust her fingers deep into the soil, the dull
sound of the snapping roots. Then she froze. There was
something solid beneath the moss.

Sabine started digging around the object. She had never seen anything like it. The white wood refused to chip beneath her nails. She scoured its grooves until it was mostly clean and then pushed her fingers into the holes to dig out the dirt, wiping it on the hip of her grey tunic. She was discovering a hollow space inside the object. Marc walked over to Sabine and she handed it to him. It was a child's skull. Large parts of the jaw were missing and most of the milk teeth were still attached. In these mud-caked gaps, a row of adult teeth had grown. Marc hung the skull above the mouth of their cabanne and the children stood side by side for a time, staring at this new addition.

Something shifted in Marc's face and he turned away from his sister and walked towards the edge of the forest. Sabine did not seem to notice. She stood blank-faced and framed by the wet dirt, the obsidian shine of secret stones, the goosefoot in green strokes, chutes of light and their drifting must. Then, very clearly, her brother's voice.

We are eating.

She nodded, but did not look up. Marc slipped through the bushes and beyond sight. After several more moments without action or thought, Sabine once again set out to harvest the forest floor. This time she was less selective, tearing away the moss in crude chunks. She sat near the newly formed pile and began kneading mud into patties.

Meanwhile Marc walked along the sun-splashed hedgerow, swatting the broom plants with his open palm and watching the yellow petals scatter in the dried mud. Soon he spotted the little ones playing in the crust of a bowl-shaped ditch. They were throwing mud rinds at each other and laughing. None of them noticed the older boy standing a few meters away, watching them with his mouth open and his tongue drying in the grim heat.

Marc would have to gather all the little ones. An infinite number of them swarmed the hedgerows. He tried to picture a fence large enough to contain them all, but each time it materialized, the children would cross its boundary and force him to begin the exercise anew. This went on for several minutes until Marc could no longer bear the sound of their joy.

His cry was lost in the hiss of the wind-whipped field, but for the children it lingered on. He could see the fear in their eyes, and this caused a blood-rush to throb in Marc's temples. He stepped forward and struck one of the children in the face with the bottom of his open palm, causing her to fall backwards into a sitting position. The flies had finally ceased their buzzing and Marc could think straight once more. From the child's nose came a thin trickle of blood.

The others watched him in silence. Marc turned and began walking away. The others helped the child to her feet and they followed Marc in single-file along the hedgerow.

Sabine was prepared. Already she had spread the straw chaff in four rough circles on the floor of their home. On each of these plates she portioned moss and mud in equal quantities.

When she had finished setting the table, Sabine stepped outside and listened for signs of Marc and the children. Nothing. She sat with her back against the trunk of a beech and closed her eyes. She could hear the slow settling of the forest, the chirruping of birds in the branches. A memory surfaced.

Her mother was setting the table. Sabine was just a baby strapped into the high chair. Her diaper was hot and wet around her. Sabine's lungs contracted and expanded with each aching sob. The kitchen was filled with blue smoke drifting from the boiling pot and up along the tile. Some of it reached the window and was pulled to wisps by the darkness.

Father entered the room and laid his hand gently on Sabine's head. The low notes of his voice shook through her body. Soon Sabine ceased crying. Mother spoke to father in short rasps. Then everyone sat down to eat. Marc was in the other high chair, quiet and smiling. Mother and father's faces were just grey smears moving up and down.

Marc looked back at the children to make sure they were

keeping pace. One of them had blood down her shirt from wiping her nose. The others fooled around as they walked. Marc hissed at them and the children fell in line and sped up. He looked back a few more times until he was satisfied with their gait. Their learning only lasted as long as the blood did. Then the children forgot and it was time to remind them again. This tired Marc.

Sabine was standing at the entrance of the cabanne, face pale and strained. Marc could tell that she had been thinking. The children walked past her and entered the dank wooden structure. Careful not to disturb anything, they took their seats around the table. The siblings stood in the doorway, blocking the light. Marc smiled and looked at the children sitting in order. Their eyes shone in the semi-darkness and he could hear them sniffling. Marc and Sabine took their places at the head of the table. Then Sabine recited the prayer.

Thank you god for this family. Please protect our health.

One of the younger children rubbed her nose and stared at her grubby fingers in the dim light, checking for blood. The little girl's parents had named her Gaëlle but she didn't know this and neither did anybody else. She watched the others chew their mud patties. Their mouths were caked with mud and she could hear the wet crunch of tiny pebbles beneath their teeth. The children grimaced as they ate. Gaëlle knew she should eat along with them if she didn't want to draw attention to herself. The two big kids with the yellow hair, they never ate. All they did was wait and watch patiently until the small ones had finished their plates. Gaëlle was just making it worse for herself by freezing up like this. She looked down at the patty and felt a warm dizziness. It was spreading from her nose to the back of her head. When the blonde boy had hit her, Gaëlle had been very warm, and the boy had pushed the warmth right into the back of her head where it had become wet and sick. Marc spoke joyfully.

Eat.

Now Sabine was watching her too. Gaëlle's saliva tasted salty and she was finding it hard to swallow. She reached for a piece of moss and put it in her mouth. Her teeth felt hollow and electric as she anticipated the crunch. Gaëlle pretended to chew, hoping the moss would become wet and disappear a little. She left it on her tongue and moved her chin up and down. Sabine whispered something to Marc and he reached over to Gaëlle's plate and broke off a piece of the mud patty. When he lifted it to her mouth, she resisted for a moment. Then Gaëlle remembered the shove Marc had given her. She opened her mouth and let him place the mud inside.

The back of her throat hardened into a knot and she was overwhelmed by nausea. Soon Gaëlle was floating up through the canopy and into the sky. There in the vaulted blue she looked over the wheat and colza running in gold and yellow strips, the scrabble of interstitial forests at the fields' edges, the unhalted woodland to the north where the maples, birches, and elms grew green and lush over the horizon. Before she knew it, the sky grew black with the beating wings of barn swallows. They jerked and swept across the ether, circling the child in a growing frenzy. Outside the cabanne Gaëlle vomited a dark mix of moss and earth. Her ribs ached and her throat burned. She wiped the vomit from her nostrils and attempted to right herself.

It was on the short walk back to the cabanne that Gaëlle heard Florian's shrieks reverberate through the trees. She turned to look but could not see the boy.

8.

Only seven children stood in the courtyard. Christophe counted them again, just to be certain. They formed a loose line, limbs restless and shifting, all waiting absent-mindedly for the old man to bathe and clothe them. But Florian was not present. Christophe looked over the squalid assembly of human shapes in his care, the reek of urine and feces, the dirty feet, the knotted hair.

Where is Florian? he said.

None of the children answered his question. He scrutinized their faces for signs of deception. Unlike these little liars, Florian had not been the product of one of Christophe's searches. Three winters ago the boy had wandered onto the farm, half-starved and on the verge of losing his toes to frostbite. Christophe had been gathering fallen leaves in the garden when he first heard the commotion. He walked around the farmhouse to find the other children standing around a hunched, naked figure in the courtyard. Some held rocks in their fists, and the boy was snarling at them. He looked wretched. By spring Christophe had nursed him back to health and chosen a name for him, but the boy's toes remained gnarled and misshapen. Soon Florian was walking again and Christophe allowed him free reign of the farmhouse. Despite the old man's attempts at disciplining the child, Florian spoke no discernible language and could only be forced to wear clothes at meal time. This was one of Christophe's inflexible rules, alongside these fortnightly washes.

The metal whistle was loud and its trill reached far into the fields and forests, but still Florian refused to appear. The old man's face remained calm as he addressed the children.

I said where is Florian?

Finally Gaëlle stepped forward. The old man did not flinch.

Yes, she said.

He looked at her. Small spasms worked their way across the

child's face. Her teeth were dark with grime.

Where?

She pointed. Christophe hissed at the children and gestured for them to stay in the courtyard. He followed Gaëlle along the dirt path, past the muddy pond and the mirabelle tree. Her gait was uneven and Christophe placed a steady hand on her shoulder. They took a left at the edge of the property where the wild heather grew in thick pink shrubs. Heat was rising from the fields in drunken fumes. Christophe noticed a thin column of smoke rising from the tree-line in the distance, but there was no time for that now. Even if they were alive, the old men were of no use to him. He did not care whether they lived or died. They could keep their eggs.

Gaëlle had stopped in her tracks and was pointing ahead. In the distance appeared the shape of a wounded animal dragging itself along the intersecting hedgerow. The child veered from left to right on his hands and knees. Christophe and Gaëlle watched Florian's limbs jolt uncontrollably. The boy collapsed and lay still for a moment, but as they neared he struggled and rose again.

Florian had severed the snake's neck and its bloody head was rolling around in his mouth. The pain had started in his cheek and shot quickly to the top of his head where it had wrapped around his neck. Now it travelled down his back like the little black stick slithering through the wild grass near the ferns. He got close as he always did, to understand, but also to drink from it. The snake had golden discs for eyes with small black slits running down the middle. Its body was the color of old leaves and wood, with dark patches of burnt soil. What's left after a fire.

So he approached the snake very slowly, his mouth in an O and his teeth making space for the kill. Of all the snakes he had hunted, this was the fastest. It wove in and out of the grass as he chased it through the trees. They reached a clearing and the snake paused. The boy crept closer and lunged. He bit the snake and the snake bit Florian, inside his mouth and through his cheek. His jaw clenched until the he felt the snake's spinal cord sever between his teeth and that's when the hurt began. Florian had never felt such pain. He fell to the forest floor and rolled onto his back. Eyes turned to the treetops, Florian saw the leaves were fangs sinking into his face through any opening possible. He tried with his eyelids to block the venom falling like bright rain from the sky. The trees were children and the children reached through his eye sockets and ate from his skull with sharp spoons, scraping for the soft tissue at the bottom of the bowl. Soon his entire body was racked with pain and his throat tightened and Florian's breathing became difficult.

Christophe could not see the fang marks, but the boy's face was bloated and his neck was no better. So it had finally happened. But all the precautions were for naught if he didn't act quickly. After a short struggle, Christophe slung Florian over his shoulder and began the journey back. This time Gaëlle had no trouble keeping up with the old man, who was considerably slowed by his burden.

The heat had left the smaller children irritable and tired. They played joylessly beneath the loose rays of waning sunlight. Lea sat hunched in the grass nearby, chewing her toenails and muttering to herself. Sabine wore no expression, the other children like fireflies adrift in the dim caverns of her consciousness. Marc slept beside her in the fetal position.

Only Lea noticed Christophe when he reappeared at the top of the path, Florian struggling fiercely in his arms. She put her shoes back on and followed them into the farmhouse.

Christophe laid the boy on the dinner table and examined his torso for puncture wounds. Florian's jaw was locked tight and he bit Christophe's fingers when the old man tried to part his lips. Christophe slapped him twice across the face and pried his teeth apart like those of a stubborn horse. This time Florian ceased struggling altogether and kept his mouth open. The slap had awakened memories of being nursed by Christophe after the long winter, and this relaxed some part of his mind.

Inside Florian's mouth Christophe found the bloody viper's head. He washed the wound with water and dried it with a rag. A single puncture. So the snake had only thrust one fang into the boy's cheek. The poison of the other, finding no flesh to pierce, had probably squirted loosely into the boy's mouth, without which Florian would already be dead.

Let us hope the vials have not gone bad, thought the old man. He had no doubt they were past their expiry date, but that didn't mean much.

Florian lost consciousness while the old man was in the cellar. He had become a thin whisper of air making its way through a swollen windpipe. He was the silken thread of a spider wriggling in the naked ether with nothing to fasten to. Already he could sense the place of shines appearing in the distance. Then from the miasma emerged the hand of some implacable being. From it a single fang and from the fang came a new venom to flood Florian with dull wet pain.

The boy was barely breathing when Christophe injected the anti-venom. Lea climbed into the soot-marked fireplace and stood there observing the dinner table, her mood affected neither by the bloody cuts on the Florian's supine body nor his terribly disfigured face. Aware of a subtle shift in his peripheral vision, Christophe turned towards her as if another snake might be lying there in wait. In Lea's face, the old man saw the expression of his wife looking down at him from the blackened stone. One of his hands remained on the boy's chest, and beneath it Florian's flesh slowly loosened as his breathing became more steady. It was the face of all women, yes, the way their eyes were set apart, but also their nose and mouth and the way all of these functioned together to make them known as themselves. Here was his wife breathing, just Lea, a child, certainly not his wife, but every wife, quite human, face peering at him, only to turn to ash and recede into a black mist.

For a single moment love had returned to suffocate the simple calm of Christophe's organized mind. False and traitorous hearts, the hearts of whores and thieves. When their time comes. How much they would suffer and in what way. If only he could... I cannot think, he thought, I cannot think and I don't know where I am. Here in the farmhouse of course. Surrounded by them. Children. I must calm myself. Make the boy drink some water when he can. Feed him well for the next few weeks. And in the meantime bathe the children, cut their nails and hair if needed, one after the other, in the usual manner, beginning with the smallest and most restless, and ending with my wife.

The old man lifted Lea out of the fireplace and when her feet touched the ground she immediately dropped to her knees and crawled beneath the dinner table. The old man's legs were purple and grey, and his face. His face again. It was the same uncertain look she remembered from the night of the soup. Lea felt the familiar vinegar spreading again through her belly. The child's face itched beneath the skin where she couldn't reach. Lea rubbed her nose and clenched her fists until her fingernails pushed into her palms and her toes curled into little balls. She crouched there in the shadows listening to the muffled sound of Christophe handling Florian's body on the table above her. Someone had bent the boy right out of shape. He was like a piece of clay rubbed in beetroot.

9.

The children fell into single file and waited to be ushered into the bathroom. Florian could not turn his head to observe this motley string of grievers, and he heard only the sound of their footsteps as they shuffled by. The boy's eyes remained open, staring fixedly at the ceiling's wooden beams, the crude white plaster hiding straw and mud, and this pain, worming its way through his marrow, out into the fingertips, and pooling in the toes, which hung like heavy black pebbles, pinning him to the table. From the next room came the sound of a small rain. Florian's hands were cold and his head blistered until it was pocked with tiny holes, all of them whistling hot air.

Christophe placed Rodolphe's soiled clothes in a wicker basket at the base of the bathtub. The boy stood squirming on the bathroom mat, limbs streaked with grime, hesitating to step over the enamel edge. But boils had been swelling where the clothes chafed his skin, and the boy knew the cold water would soothe these.

Christophe watched Rodolphe climb into the tub, this one always wincing at first, but after a few gasping breaths complaining very little. Christophe soaked and lathered the washcloth before scrubbing the boy. Rodolphe gritted his teeth and held the side of the tub with both hands.

Sit down, said the old man.

And Rodolphe did, feeling the cold enamel beneath his buttocks as he leaned forward to let the old man wash his hair. After a thorough rinsing, Rodolophe stood shivering in silence as the old man dried him, clipped his toenails and fingernails, brushed his teeth, and clothed the boy.

Now go, said the old man.

Rodolphe did not hesitate. Out in the courtyard a breeze combed through his damp hair, filling his belly with a wobbling joy. Christophe looked over the remaining children to make sure nobody had disturbed Florian. He pressed his ear to the boy's chest and listened to his breathing. Improvement. The swelling seemed to be subsiding. The old man walked into the kitchen and poured a glass of water, forcing the boy to drink most it. Likely the child would survive. Christophe passed his hand back and forth in front of the Florian's eyes. They did not move. Let us hope the venom has not caused any permanent damage to his system. The old man did not want to think of what he would have to do if Florian were to lose his eyesight.

That night a full moon rose over the farmhouse, and the shingles shone blue where a century of rain had streaked slime across the roofing. In the courtyard grass grew sparsely between the stones, spreading in fading rings from the lone sapling at its center. From the pond came the anguished croaks of frogs attempting to couple. They crouched in the moonlight, bodies shining wetly, eyes black and unresolved. Inside the abandoned building across the courtyard rats could be heard burrowing through the moldy grain vats. On the upper floor of the farmhouse, the children slept in two rows of cots filling a single room, some snoring and others simply with their mouths open, curled in the fetal position beneath the sheets, or with their limbs splayed, having kicked the bedding to the floor.

Lea could not sleep. She lay on her back watching the moon through the square skylight and listened to Florian's labored breath. He had kissed the world and the world had kissed him back. It was punishment, but for what? The boy's eyes were open, but they refused her gaze. A world without eyes, she thought to herself, is not a good world. And now Christophe had confiscated her dress, and for how long? She had only torn it a little.

In the gloom of half-sleep, Marc felt his father's hand holding him by the collar, squeezing his soft neck as he pulled him back onto the sidewalk. The cars screamed past, one after the other, their hard surfaces reflecting the buildings and streetlights.

Sabine and mother were not there that day. It was Marc and father alone in the city. What are you doing, you little piece of scum, his father shouted. Then after the light had turned green and they had crossed the street, squeezing his hand until it hurt, father kneeled, his face appearing as big as a building. I'm sorry Marc, dad should not have used those words, but you scared him, understand.

Then Sabine was smiling at Marc, because everything had gone so quiet. There were three men in the apartment and Marc couldn't do anything. Mother and father were gone. He felt the boot against his chest, holding him down, the sound of a bird very scared, and Sabine smiling because of the quiet, and the men leaving, how they looked tired and dirty, and her breathing not very far away, and his breathing also, and the night, long and black.

10.

Florian watched the light. It shone a deeper yellow as the days grew shorter. Always it made its way across the room, over the beds of the smaller children where it first appeared in the morning, across his sheets in a hot yellow square, shifting up the mud-lime wall, illuminating bits of straw between the beams, to flatten there and mysteriously disappear. The ceiling was slanted in sections like the dark red skin of a fish and it got darker and heavier once the gold was gone. What remained in the room was a different kind of light, blue and aimless, with no fire whatsoever, and so without interest to Florian.

The snake had left more snakes. They were under his bed, making their little tongues disappear and whispering softly to one another. They could not climb the bed, they could not climb the bed, they could not. The room was snakeless. But sometimes he heard them slithering under his bed in a great pit. The other children fed them dead rats to keep them alive. He knew this to be true. And sometimes when nobody was around, no child and no sound, Florian flopped onto his belly and dragged himself to the edge of the mattress, where he hung his head over the edge and peered beneath the bed at the dust balls on the moldy carpeting. Florian would then crawl back to his previous position, arranging his body to match the shape of his pain.

Every night the children joined him in his creaking upper room and filled it with noise. Christophe rarely appeared. He did not like to interfere. Lea used these few minutes before bedtime to stare at Florian. The boy could hear her quiet sounds, like wind blowing through open eaves, and he was surprised by his desire to touch her, which came immense and overwhelming. This was something entirely new for the boy, as Florian usually avoided contact with his kind. Over and over he would picture the movement, the way his hand might reach through the air and touch hers, but in his mind he could see a great wall of snakes frozen together and sleeping like fish in a lake, and so Florian did not move and Lea stood there staring, fingers bent, knocking her nails together. Then Christophe's footsteps could be heard coming from the dining room and he yelled up the stairs.

Bedtime, he said.

Once the candles were blown and the quiet returned, Florian watched the bat as it flew from beam to beam in the darkness. The boy squirmed in silence, careful not to wake the others.

11.

Rodolphe stood in the courtyard throwing stones at the cement wall. He enjoyed the sharp sound this produced, the fading echo, the pain in his shoulder. Images of Marc's face appeared and dissolved into pulsing yellow dots, eyes opening and closing, now aiming for the metal ring hanging from a hole in the cement. When finally he struck it, a sound like a bird's chirp ricocheted into the eaves of the farmhouse. To Florian lying in bed, it rang out in the mist of his half-dream, dispersing the snakes in a slithering frenzy. Still the boy did not wake until the sound of Christophe's steps grew louder, a sound he had learned to detect even in a state of deep slumber and that signified only one thing: danger. If the old man found out that Florian could crawl to the edge of the bed, walk even, he might force him to his feet and out into the world where he would surely be swallowed and perish.

Christophe stood over Florian and watched him tremble. He slipped his arms beneath the boy's body and carried him slowly down the stairs, teetering back and forth to stay balanced on the smooth wooden steps, careful not to fall and break his coccyx, for that would truly be the end. Afterwards the old man rested for a moment, sitting on the lowest step and holding the boy in his lap, fairly reeking of piss and looking truly forlorn, with his arms and legs very thin and his prick hanging between his legs like a solitary worm. The old man's face was expressionless and his eyeballs seemed to retract into his skull as he observed the boy.

There was a natural order to things.

Not first in the bathtub, of course. He shook his head.

Now the boy was sitting on the toilet shivering wet, and that was because Christophe had not respected the reality of things. Florian struggled to loosen his bowels, muscles pale and stiff, rigid with effort. When the boy had finished, Christophe put him back in the tub.

A solution for the soiled sheets, a permanent one. After several weeks of daily washes, the old man's back was in a certain amount of pain. He had considered letting the boy lie in his own filth, but had seen the boils people developed from lying in unclean beds and they were another matter altogether, worse even than urine and feces. He had no desire to clean pus or administer additional medicine.

The water ran clear. Christophe sat Florian on the edge of the tub and dried his upper body. He pulled the boy up and held him at the waist, drying his lower body with his free hand. Lea peered into the bathroom through the small window and watched them. Dancers: the older one, clothed in simple cotton rags, bowing before his partner. The other, thin and naked, hanging from his embrace.

12.

Christophe carried the boy upstairs and lay him on the freshly-made cot. His hair was still wet and Christophe thought he could see the boy peering through his parted eyelids. The old man stood over the little liar and watched Florian's eyelids flutter and press together. He watched his own hand reach out and slap him across the face. Now his cheek was red and the child had learned a valuable lesson. Your hand is my hand, thought the old man. That hand was mine. I have hurt the child. Nonsense, he thought, the child is unconscious and does not realize what happened. But you do. Yes I do, thought the old man, and felt profoundly unhappy. He pulled the sheet over the boy as if to disguise his act.

Through the skylight a dull light crept, filling the room with shadows. The old man placed the milk jug at the foot of the child's bed. Between the streaks of rust, its surface shone azure like a beetle's shell. Christophe unwound the length of garden hose and made sure the rubber band was secured. He tied a length of string around the boy's waist and ran the hose off the end of the bed and into the milk jug, where the boy's urine was to collect. I must instruct the other children to stay away from this contraption, Christophe thought.

The dinner table was covered in filthy cutlery and dishes, flies standing atop morsels of dried porridge. The old man watched one of the insects as it rubbed its legs together and looked in no discernible direction. In the courtyard, an angry child continued to throw stones. Christophe walked through the kitchen and opened a drawer. From it he removed two batteries, relics now, these small metal cylinders wrapped in colorful plastic. He rolled them back and forth between his palms until the batteries felt warm, then inserted them into the portable compact-disc player. Not his last two, but close.

The usual disc was already inside. He removed the headphones from the drawer and placed them over his ears, appreciating the quiet this produced. The old man sat in his chair with the device balanced on his bony thighs. Slowly, he closed his eyes and allowed the music to take its place, populating the darkness in its sparse and mournful way.

When Christophe disassembled the music and returned it to the drawer, the boy had ceased throwing rocks in the courtyard. None of the children could be heard. He noticed the leaves had begun to fall from the sapling, each of them a very specific shape and color, most long, thin, a shade of orange, scattered on the grass, forming no pile, meager and deformed. Young. He knew this marked the beginning of autumn, the tired season, so humid that the bones of the old ached terribly, a season shaken into the tree by the cruel hands of children and lasting longer than any other.

He looked out the window, down through that molten deformation the years had caused. In the thickness of the pane where all was warped, there came another change in the old man's mind. Glass is dust, he thought, sucked from the earth and heated, in the same way we paint a corpse to forget its true nature, and transparent only by name. Christophe heard the voice of his wife.

Just for tonight, she said, and looked at him with a hopeful quake in her eyes, dissolving at the edges.

He stood halfway between the doorway and the bed, watching her on the bed, his wife's resolve built from the flimsiest of materials, before he leaned through the silence to take his pillow, one knee propped on the bed, smelling her indefinable scent like that of dried berries, then sliding open the drawer beneath the bed and carrying the spare bedding into the living room, sinking, sinking where his ribs held together, as water collapses dust.

Christophe had slept crumpled on the sofa for a month and three days before he purchased a military bed in a surplus store near Gambetta, built of square aluminum tubing and dark grey polyester, permanent enough to accommodate his entire body, but foldable with the hope that his wife might change her mind, as if her mind were the only barrier to their reconciliation. He set it up in his office, perpendicular to the desk, and his wife never mentioned its purchase. They continued to work together in the store, her attending to the thinning stream of customers, him cleaning the floors, restocking the bins, wiping the counters, vacuuming, receiving the increasingly erratic deliveries, carrying the boxes from room to room. None of the customers noticed a difference. Most were too worried with their own problems, and anyways they had always thought Christophe was some sort of employee, as his tasks showed no sign of ownership.

He touched her in the evenings, when his mind set itself on pleasing her, which he went about systematically. After she angled his mouth correctly and achieved a dry orgasm, he would slide up and kiss her once on the mouth, then place his lips on her neck as he entered her, thrusting a dozen times, saying I'm going to come, and her simply responding, fill me, until he did and they lay still for some moments, in union.

Then even this daily ritual ceased, replaced by the hard military bed, and her alone in the bedroom, limbs spread to meet the empty space, and him wondering what if anything had altered. We should leave the city as soon as possible, Christophe, but he would not leave the store, and he would not leave Paris, and anyways the accounts were exaggerated to catch people's attention and profit from the resulting panic. He was a stubborn fool but she could not bring herself to leave him there alone.

In this manner, and despite not delivering the killing blow, Christophe caused his wife's death.

She no longer loved me, said the old man to the window. These are the daydreams of a foolish child. But he could hear her cracked voice and see her long uncombed hair, and her burst open eye, and the white liquid oozing from where the other eyeball had been pushed into a slant, so she looked away like a fish. His dead wife with the soles of her sneakers barely scuffed, the sneakers he had found in the Marais, among the empty shoeboxes and thick chunks of broken glass. They're comfortable, she had said, and smiled at him. That night he had slept soundly on the military bed, a cold breeze coming through the window of the office, and Paris was quiet. Not even a car in the streets, just the sound of gunshots at dawn, closer together and breaking the silence now, echoing down the narrow streets and up into the window, until the old man awoke in a sweat. He was lying on the sofa in the farmhouse.

Christophe looked into the fireplace where Lea had stood the day before. It was empty. The stone was shining where no soot covered it, and the sounds continued. He rose from the sofa and walked to the window. The boy was throwing rocks again. Then, after a few throws, Rodolphe did not lean over to pick up the next stone. His head was bobbing up and down. He began spinning his arms like propellers. Soon the boy was running around the courtyard, face red, eyes wide and vacant, shoes raising dust, lips vibrating to the sound of a motor.

13.

Other children slapped their palms together in a pattern. These children are playing games, fed with this food to play more games, and anyways they have no future, thought the old man. But who are these children. I don't recognize them. Of course you do. Look at them closely. There is the skin that blisters, the angry one, there is the one who led you to Florian, snot hanging from bedraggled hair, there is the one whose eyes are too close together, and there is the one who smashed the teapot like a careless twit. You know each of these children. You are the one who feeds them as you starve. God will provide our weakness what it needs to survive. These aren't just words. He is calling us to his breast. This may even be his plan for us. To play games in the grass. To be obliterated or fed. He speaks to us in this life. We are fed and so we do not starve. Starving children do not listen to their father. They listen only to their bellies. Once they have heard the words of their father, you may bury these children. Then you will be fed.

The children will not be fed because Lucien and Joseph are hoarding the eggs. For a long time they were good neighbors. They lived alone with their chickens and single rooster, a rachitic animal. They lived in the home that their father built, the two old men who were also brothers. I would bring vegetables from the garden and they would give me fresh eggs from their hens. They even had wine in the cellar, the entrance to which was concealed beneath a moldy persian carpet, ancient hunting scene. They liked to tell the story of how their father's father had hidden jews down there.

Bloated old crabs really, and gutless. Eating eggs together in that musty little home, growing old and limp. Lucien and Joseph raped and killed my wife. They took her eggs and we had no children. They kept her eggs warm in their home. The two old men sat on her eggs to keep them warm. They squatted over the eggs and kept them pressed to their warm assholes once the last hen died. They poked a hole in the egg and sucked the yolk right through. The children were born inside their bellies to walk the earth after the old men finally passed away. Lucien and Joseph are alive. Your wife was infertile. Your wife was like an egg with naught but white. When they poked her open, Lucien and Joseph sucked the empty fluid right out.

This time the old man was on his knees, holding a pillow to his chest, and once again he did not know how he had arrived there. The window was dangerous, a place of chaos. Carefully he stood. The room had not changed. He found the watch on the kitchen counter near the window. Lunchtime. No wonder the children were gathered on the grass at the center of the courtyard. The old man walked through the dining room and opened the front door. Lea was sitting quietly off to the side, watching the other children play. She saw the old man appear, stand for a moment, look down, and close the door. She had never seen his grey chest before: a dull coat of armor across which vaporous scores of white hair rose like scars from a curved blade. She pushed her own hair to her nose and inhaled deeply, sucking her thumb through the messy strands. Lea tried with her actions to restore order, but the children were too noisy. She bunched her hair into her eyes until everything went black, but still Lea could hear the other children and see Christophe standing in the doorway in his underwear and socks, a look of great confusion disfiguring the old man before he disappeared again.

Christophe found his clothes folded in a neat pile beside the sofa. He put on his pants and tightened his belt. He had lost a notch in the last six months. The old man walked into the kitchen and opened the doors to the pantry. There he found a plastic bucket full of dirt-caked potatoes. Grunting and bending his knees, the old man lifted the bucket, set it on the counter, and tilted it into the sink. The potatoes rolled out in a great fracas, their thuds hollow against the thin metal. The old man was drawing short breaths. The pipes creaked as he opened the tap and then hissed as the water ran. His bare hands twisted around the potato as he scrubbed. The dirt ran off his fingers and into the sink, where it shored up against the other potatoes or was dragged along the metal and into the drain. A wasteful process. Usually he would have filled the bottom of the bucket with some water and scrubbed the potatoes there. But Christophe needed the white noise. He did not trust his own mind.

Stuck to the side of the third potato was a layer of mud and sediment that refused to soften in the stream. The old man chipped at it with his fingernails. Soon the potato's skin was flapping loosely beneath the running water. The yellow flesh was uncovered and Christophe knew the wound was porous. The potato soaked up the water until it became fat and spongy. Christophe stared at it for a moment before he turned off the tap. He looked at the remaining potatoes, muddy and glistening in the sink. Two clean potatoes on the counter. He tried to squeeze the waterlogged tuber but it felt as hard as a rock. He had seen it grow in volume. The water had penetrated. The potato had swollen. He placed it next to the other clean potatoes on the counter. He did not look at it. Instead he opened the tap again and resumed scrubbing. The other potatoes did not show any such signs.

When he was finished Christophe wiped his hands on a rag and retrieved the cast-iron pot from its hanging place on the wooden beam. He filled it with water and turned on the gas. Christophe covered the pot. He did not look out the window. He did not look at the clean potatoes. He stood over the pot and listened to the rising sound of the water until he felt confident that it was boiling. Then he removed the pot top and dropped the potatoes in one by one, focusing his attention on the blistering water as it built to froth. Soon he would feed the children. They had been waiting long enough.

Lea had been watching the doorway. When finally the old man reappeared, she uncovered her face to better observe him. He walked out into the courtyard, wearing familiar clothes. Two of the small ones had been tumbling around on the grass and they froze in strange positions to observe the old man. He was approaching slowly, with an unsteady lilt. All of the children had stopped now, watching Christophe. After a few steps on the grass the old man slowly bent his knees and lowered himself to the ground. There he sat among the leaves and the children, hands locked together and hunched forward.

After a long period of quiet scored only by the distant cry of a bird, Lea was the first to move. She walked uncertainly over to the old man, whose head had dipped until his face was obscured. She stood behind his back and wrapped her arms partway around his torso. Like this Lea held Christophe. The old man was crying and she felt his silent convulsions in her own body. The other children watched the old man and the girl. Their limbs relaxed but they did not move. Then Sabine's fingers began searching through the grass for some insect or worm. Some of the children's eyes darted back and forth from Sabine to Lea. Nobody had ever touched the old man like this. Their faces were flush with embarrassment and several of them squirmed and pulled nervously at the crotch of their jumpsuits. Marc's upper lip receded. His teeth were visible and he sat transfixed by the scene. Even the sound of his sister's fingers did not distract him. Marc's stomach was filled with something hard and cold.

Christophe shifted his torso until Lea's fingers loosened and her arms loosened and she stepped back. He lifted his head and looked around at the other children. Then he rose to his feet with a grunt and stood there half-composed. Still the girl stood a few paces behind him, with her little fingers wriggling and her arms in the shape of a crescent, as if she were waiting for the old man to return to his previous position. Marc wanted to smash a piece of wood across her arms and pull out her eyeballs. Sabine was chewing on something slowly, her eyes lost in the middle distance. The other children watched the old man. His shoulders were stiff and his face was severe and grey.

He turned around and looked at Lea. His shoulders slumped and his face softened imperceptibly.

Stay here, he said. All of you stay here.

We are eating, asked Gaëlle.

Yes, we are eating, said Christophe. Stay here.

Gaëlle's mouth hung open as she considered the situation. They were eating, she thought, but the old man had forbidden her to follow him to the usual place. She didn't want to bother him again, for fear that he might become angry and deprive her of food. Gaëlle was starving. All she had eaten that day was a slug Sabine had fed her, which she had vomited most of. She hoped the old man had not prepared a meal of mud and moss. Her throat was rancid. She had drunk some water from the pond but it only carried the taste farther down her neck. It was burning the sides of her throat and she couldn't scratch it away.

Gaëlle's hair fell dark and stringy over her face and through it her blue eyes shone. Her mouth, wide and protruding, simian almost, seemed to undulate in some unseen current, with her tongue coiling madly beneath it and sliding across her lips. Her cheeks were smeared with gleaming slime trails. The child had thin legs, thin arms, and a thin neck.

Sabine picked up a leaf and began meticulously plucking the flesh from it, keeping the veins intact, staring closely at her work until what remained resembled a skeletal candelabrum. She held the stem and twirled it between her thumb and index finger. The shadow cast by the sapling was making its way across the blue cloth of her jumpsuit, creased and jagged, and when she leaned forward it seemed to leap to her face and straighten. There it remained, drawn diagonally across one of her eyes, until she moved again, deliberately, her face like a pale brown mask beneath which her blue veins mapped another world.

Marc's nipples were swollen. They were purple and filled with a watery ache. He was careful to keep his jumpsuit zipped and reveal nothing of this to the other children. Not even Sabine knew about this new weakness. Nor did she know about his hanging sack, where previously the pain had come only from violence. Sabine sometimes kicked him down there. Not often, but when she did the pain was worse than anything. Now there was a new pain. It came from nothing at all, just a dull and forceful swelling with no origin except his own body. A new hardness too, with hot flesh to push between his knuckles until it became a kind of pleasure. It scared Marc. He could feel it worming its way into his strength and turning his ideas soft. So when the pleasure came Marc would force his prick between his closed fists until the pain made it small and soft again. At night his bones ached as they grew. He was made of the same wet wood as the cabanne in the forest. Marc stared at the farmhouse and rubbed the small hairs on his upper lip until they burned. Then he closed his fist, walked across the grass, and punched Lea in the small of the back.

She fell onto her hands and knees in silence. The younger children gathered around and touched her back, as if to exorcise the pain they had all known. Unaware of these worshipping pilgrims, Lea did not move, focusing instead on the pain twisting along her spine. Marc returned to his sister and sat by her side. She paid him no attention but instead planted the stem of the third stripped leaf into the soil and began working on a fourth. Sabine stared at her fingers in dull concentration as she worked. Marc looked grimly at her miniature forest. Then he looked at her. No matter how long he pressed his body to hers, how hard he gripped her fingers, how much he looked into the pit of her eyes, how many homes built in the forest, meals served together, nights spent looking at her as she slept, or holding her as she woke in terror from dreams, this sister was no longer human and she never would be again. She was the dark paint strewn across the sky to mask the stars, the blood spilled from a wound. Sabine had died that day in the apartment and Marc could never retrieve her.

The olive oil fell in a golden rivulet through the rising steam. The old man pushed down with the masher, rending the skin and collapsing the soft flesh of the potatoes until they were unrecognizable. The raw garlic was tougher, and he could feel each bulb explode beneath the masher. He should have diced it at the very least. The farmhouse was a collapsing structure barely held together by years of human effort. Christophe had long since abandoned any sealing work. The mud-lime dated back to the early nineteen-hundreds. There was nothing to be done. These would be meager portions. He added more olive oil, salted the mash and stirred it with a silver serving spoon. With the bowls in two stacks on a tray beside nine spoons and a clean folded rag, Christophe walked out into the courtyard.

Lea had ceased crying and she joined the other children as they observed the stone god's face behind a thin curtain of rising steam, every imperceptible movement an omen of his grace or wrath. A quiet reverence fell over the courtyard. The old man placed a bowl and spoon in front of each child. Therein he portioned an equal amount of mash. When all the children were served, he sat in the grass and spoke.

Eat.

The children looked at each other, suspicious that the old man had not yet prayed or served himself. Then one by one, sensing that their safety might be guaranteed, they lifted the spoons to their mouths. Christophe scraped the bottom of the cast-iron pot and served himself what remained, approximately half of what each child had received. He sat cross-legged and ate on the grass, his limbs relatively loose, looking over his children. Molten bronze beneath the sun, scattered there like so many loose leaves. After a few mouthfuls, the old man let his spoon rest in the bowl. A smile deformed his grey face. It was brimming with grief and joy concurrent, twisting together like two sides of an eddy.

14.

Born of the autumn sludge, between the fallen leaves, a damp stench rose from the forest floor. The mushrooms pushed through this placental layer, and from it small plants drew strength, bowing to the sun's arc, ever striving with their delicate leaves to find some bit of stray nourishment shining through the brilliant canopy. Every few days, and for varying periods, a consolidating rain would fall. It beat steadily at the treetops, streaming down the branches and trunks to settle the quiet soil. In the rainless periods, when the clouds hung motionless or dissipated altogether, small creatures could be heard scurrying nervously through the dry leaves.

Rodolphe squatted over the edge of the pond with a stick in one hand. Fastened to its extremity was a length of fishing line, and from it dangled a piece of shredded plastic. This unfamiliar insect floated back and forth in front of the frogs, who sat calmly on the muddy shelves above the water, unmoving but for their eyeballs rolling to and fro in their sockets.

This fly made no sound. It had no wings to make a sound.

It was in fact the hand and rifle of a plastic soldier Rodolphe had found half-buried in the ground two weeks prior. There had been several full soldiers too, and in the dark crawlspace above the grain vats Rodolphe had used rat turds and dried wheat to build sandbags and foxholes, pitting the men against each other in a series of grim, lifeless conflicts.

The frogs stared at the plastic rifle as it swung from left to right. Light green and mottled, the leaves of the weeping willow could be seen reflected in the black center of their gold-rimmed eyes. Rodolphe's shoulders were rigid and hunched, his mouth forming a small O as he concentrated on his prey.

When finally the frog leapt, Rodolphe pulled his stick violently upward and flung it high into the air, its legs and arms outstretched and flailing wildly until it landed with a wet thud among the wheat stalks. Rodolphe screamed and bolted towards the edge of the field where he stood squinting, seeking. And there it was, hopping broken-legged through the stalk shadows. Turning it over, he used the tip of his finger to stroke the frog's belly in small circles, but it refused to sleep. He could feel its heart beating through the viscous white skin as he walked along the edge of the pond, spine straight, all the way back to the courtyard where he delivered the creature.

Splayed across the easternmost section of the courtyard lay the dust-caked organs of several small animals. When Rodolphe appeared with the frog, the other children screamed and rushed around him with their hands outstretched, each wanting to hold it before the others. They tore the frog open and examined its beating heart, standing open-palmed and wide-eyed, pulling at its ropy intestine until it came unraveled completely. Rodolphe was the center of this excited joy and his cheeks burned red with pride. He was round and short and tough, with thick brown eyebrows hanging over his eyes, and the bottom of his jaw protruding roundly so that his smile looked idiotic and reassuring.

Lea had ridden out farther than ever. Turning right on the departementale, the bicycle had carried her along the road, black and long, splitting the green fields and abandoned farms, pressed down by the sky, a heavy grey dome that seemed made of cement. Yes she was nowhere now, and the air felt thick and moist, pressing her jumpsuit to her tired legs. The tears had stopped after the second uphill, and soon she was far away from Florian's dead body, the way his chest heaved against the sheets and that awful machine stealing his piss every day and night.

Lea stood atop the hill looking down at the road ahead, and the road behind, with nothing recognizable, and rain swelling in the black clouds overhead. Two hills away she could see a tall, thin structure piercing the smudged horizon. Lea wondered what could possibly be inside. A place away from the rain. A dry place. She got back on the bicycle and started pedaling, a furious sign of life on a long, dead road.

The sky sputtered and rumbled, and soon small tendrils of lightning could be seen reaching from the clouds down into the forestlands. Lea gripped the handlebars to avoid getting sucked up into the sky. Her limbs were thin and hollow like an ant's, and she feared being torn apart, each limb plucked from her and spread by the wind like so many dandelion seeds. The rain began falling in small drops at first, but before long it grew heavy, pushed slantwise by the storm.

Before Lea cleared the first hill, she was entirely soaked and could only hear the deep growl of thunder filling the air and surrounding her, angry, whispering as the men do between clenched teeth, when—crack—lightning struck an elm to her right, going unnoticed so hard was Lea's struggle to keep the bicycle moving up the incline. High also spun the arcs of water flung from her tires, splashing Lea's back and lost in the general flooding of her person, wheels barely splitting the water anymore, and Lea's hair now matted to her head, mouth open to reveal her bottom teeth trembling, chattering.

Clearing the hill she began to gain speed, downslope with her stomach getting smaller and her feet pedaling into the endless vacuum ahead and below. The wobbling was now so intense that it flung her little body from side to side. Lea screamed until her voice lost its human qualities, forming alongside the droning rain a shrill mono-syllable like that of an industrial saw, open mouth filling with rain water, eyes epileptic. Instinctively the child began to assume fetal position as the bicycle swerved right and the front tire struck a milestone, and again Lea was flung through the air, this time into a rain-filled ditch, where her open mouth was instantly flooded with muddy water, rotten weeds, and insects. Underwater she struggled to find footing, clawing with her hands and feet at the soft mire, until finally she managed to emerge from the ditch, sputtering filth from her still-screaming mouth, a nightmarish apparition, a childish golem scrambling up the bank and onto the road where she collapsed, unhurt, crying and screaming as the rain began to wash her.

After a long fit of coughing, Lea vomited brown water and began unzipping her jumpsuit. She resembled a snake molting clumsily in the middle of the road until finally the child had kicked free of the muddy clothing. The storm drains were clogged and the water rose steadily but Lea did not hurry to her feet, opting instead to lay naked on her back and stare at the sky. Behind the clouds a blue fire raged calmly, thunder lost in the rainfall. Heat slowly drained from her body. The cold would carry her if she stopped fighting. It had been there before her, and it would remain after she was gone. The choice was not hers.

Fists balled, she rolled onto her stomach and struggled onto her hands and knees. Her hair like a black shroud fallen about her face, the sound of her wild breath existing only as an echo in that nascent darkness. Burning cheeks. Aching eyes. The bicycle. She could see flashes of rust in the flooded ditch and this caused her to rise uneasily and scramble towards it. Fingers curled between the spokes, Lea pulled the front wheel with all her might, leaning backwards, feet scraping on the wet asphalt until the machine began slowly moving through the water. The veins in her neck bulged and she was making slow progress when she lost her footing, slipped, and disappeared beneath the waterline. Her fingers continued to grip the wheel and Lea held her breath, careful not to inhale any more water. Quickly she rose again. Making sharp little noises, teeth bared, eyes squinting, rain beating around her small shape, Lea dragged the bicycle from the ditch and into the shallows. Knowing the hardest part was now behind her, the child sat in the slow-moving water to catch her breath, one hand resting on the wheel, afraid the bicycle might be carried off again to disappear into what seemed like an ocean come to swallow everything. The faint outline of a smile was visible between the long black strands of her wet hair.

Soon the rain lessened and fissures of blue-grey light appeared in the cloud cover. The thunder came sparsely now and the lightning had receded into the distance, blanching the horizon at ever-widening intervals. When she no longer felt the bike might float away, Lea rose and picked up the jumpsuit, wrung it out, and slung it over her bare shoulder. She pushed the bicycle upright and held the handlebars as she rolled it up the hill.

It was no castle. When it came into view again, Lea could see it was just a tower at the top of the hill, an ordinary cylinder of grey cement stuck there by the side of the road, covered in black graffiti. Lea propped her bicycle against the side of the windowless structure and walked back onto the road. A cement path led to a door at the base of the tower. Rain trickled down the sanded metal. It shone like the inside of an oyster shell, and Lea stood transfixed by the streaking light. The handle was thin and sharp, hurting Lea's hands as she pulled with no results. Eventually and after much stubborn effort, the door swung on its hinges, emitting a long and plaintive sound. The darkness inside was absolute. Lea stood at the threshold of this black place and dared not cross it. The door felt hard and cold on her shoulder blades, but Lea refused to let it push her inside. She pressed her hair to her nose but it was too wet to provide any comfort, so she suckled on the cold tips of her fingers and squatted in the doorway, staring into the darkness, holding the door ajar with her lower back, half-expecting Christophe to appear. Small glints here and there. The sound of chafing cloth. Lea held three fingers in her mouth. Slowly her eyes began to adapt to the darkness and she could see many objects gleaming at foot-level, and a staircase leading up to a second floor, sketched in faded gold, then undulating brightly until a shape appeared, a candle floating in the darkness, and the hand clutching it: ancient, thin, pale. Behind the candle a face with no eyebrows, framed in filthy grey hair, two eyes very wide, and a mouth like a small prune. The old woman stood in the stairway, smiling at the child.

My fat little one, she said to Lea. You're cold, you. Come and warm up.

She spoke with two voices, one a high-pitched squeal, the other a blunt rasp. One was contained in the other, enveloped, like a thin wire pushed through a tough piece of gristle. Lea was not scared of the old woman. She did not listen to her words but relied exclusively on instinct, and Lea's body felt unthreatened by the frail and nervous figure standing before her. She stepped into the room and the door closed behind her. An intense vinegary smell emanated from the hundreds of empty wine bottles scattered throughout the room. Only a rough path from the door to the stairway lay outlined between their shining shapes.

I'll get you a blanket.

The old woman disappeared up the stairs. The candlelight faded until Lea could barely see anything. The ghostly shapes of bottles. A stairway, faintly shimmering. The sharp edges of metal cabinets against the right wall. When the old woman returned, she was carrying a wool blanket over one arm, and she held the candle in the other, and once more the bottles seemed to dance in the golden light. Lea walked slowly through them, eyes focused downwards, careful not to kick any of them over. When she reached the base of the stairs she stood at arm's length from the old woman, and extended her open palm. The old woman handed her the blanket and took the wet jumpsuit from the child's shoulder. Lea barely noticed. The blanket was made of wool, and it made her skin prickle, but she did not complain and wrapped herself in it, shivering and staring at the old woman, who started up the steps without looking back.

Come. I'll dry this for you. Come up. It's warmer here.

The old woman blew out the candle when she reached the top of the stairs. The golden light vanished, replaced by a grey gloom emanating from a grid-shaped skylight. Torn wires hung from dark holes in the wall, where the dusty outlines of long-absent machinery remained etched. Glass bottles stacked horizontally, heavy with black liquid, and stacks of cans, their labels printed with images of corn, fish, lentils, sausages, carrots, peas, and dog food. A filthy mattress lay against the wall with a single pillow propped up on it. A plastic lawn chair. In the far right corner of the room, a narrow metal staircase led to a trapdoor in the ceiling. The old woman hung the jumpsuit over one of the steps. She looked at Lea and smiled again, exposing the wide gaps between her purple teeth.

They turned the electricity off. I told them I need it, gonna burn the place down with these candles. You know what they said.

She sat in the lawn chair, legs up, one hand on the armrest, the other tilting a bottle to her lips, drinking wine, spilling some on her dress, a blue flower pattern, or what was left of it. Lea stood in the middle of the room shivering, holding the blanket around her body, bunching it to her nose and sniffing the damp mold, less sharp than the smell coming from the empty bottles.

Come on. Sit on the mattress, my fat little one. It's for you. It will dry. It always dries. You can't just wait like an idiot. You have to lie down. You have to sit. You have to rest, it's important to rest.

Lea looked at the mattress and looked at the old woman. She did as she was told, sitting against the wall with her knees pulled up to her chin, small head protruding from the blanket like smoke from a teepee.

The doctor told me to keep warm and drink wine, it's cheaper than pills. For the pain. I have terrible pain all over my body. I have terrible terrible pain. The worst is at night. That's the worst. When it's cold. The doctor said wine. I have epilepsy. My husband couldn't take it anymore. He shot himself right in the mouth. He couldn't take me anymore. But I wasn't dead. He missed me. He shot himself and he missed me. It was dark. I stayed quiet. I didn't say anything. Then when he shot himself I got up. I had two pellets in the back of my neck and my ear was missing. I couldn't feel anything. I just heard the shot, whining and whining, only thing I could hear. He couldn't handle the epilepsy. Said you stop flopping around like that. I surprised myself by not moving. If he had seen me. I didn't move. I work all day, don't need to work at night too, here's a piece of wood to put in your mouth. You keep going like that we'll have to call the hospital. Like an old goat. Bite this. They'll take you away for good. What a brute. It's epilepsy, I told him. He didn't listen, he never listened. He was a real drinker my husband. I don't drink alcohol, only wine. But he used to drink a bathtub of vodka every night. I can still hear through this hole in my head, but not where the sound is coming from. That's the other ear. My friend Laurence told me he had cancer. Then why didn't he tell me himself. His wife. His own wife. I knew what they did because of her face. He killed himself to save you from seeing him like that, she told me, but why in god's name did he shoot my ear off. Ask his doctor. No answer, the doctor. A first-rate whore. I wore white. My head was wrapped in white, which was good for him, in the end. What he deserved. But I suppose it could have been me, the funeral, lying against his blown-off head. They kept the casket closed but everybody threw roses on the casket. I should have given her a slap. She cried at the funeral. I didn't cry. I bought a cat.

The old woman drank from the bottle and smiled at Lea, who stared at this new creature, one whose words fell out like water from a tap, and without any meaning, or too fast to understand, so that Lea listened only to their rhythm, which she found pleasant and soothing.

Nobody has the right to take their own life. We should not tell the universe when and where we live or die. My husband is an idiot. What do you think about that, my little fat one. Not much. Too young to think about it. Once you reach a certain age it starts coming more naturally. You think of death. You think of the past. They'll say many things. You tell them what to do. It's the only way to deal with them. You'll stay pretty for longer if you tell them what to do. Are you warm yet. You stopped trembling my little flea. It's cold out there. It looks like you stopped trembling. It's warmer in here.

The old woman took another swig from the bottle and put it back down. She rose and produced a penknife from the pocket of her dress. She opened it and stumbled around the room, knife forward, towards Lea, then turning around, remembering something, mumbling to herself, and walking towards the canned food. Lea did not feel any fear. She sat immobile and watching the old woman as she used the penknife to pry open a can of tuna. The sound of the knife splitting the can, causing Lea's teeth to grind and her toes to squirm. The old woman held out the can, and Lea leaned forward to sniff the tuna. She pulled back and held the blanket to her nose again.

No. Well I suppose it's not for everyone, fish. I used to cook a lot. No gas here. No gas.

She laughed for a long time before interrupting herself.

But if you want anything…

The old woman gestured to the other cans with the knife.

You just tell me. You tell me and I'll take care of it.

She tipped the can of tuna into her mouth and chewed the pieces tumbling through the gashed metal, sucking the water, flecks falling onto her dress, and a trickle running down her chin. Lea stared at the old woman's foot: it was wrapped in filthy blackened gauze.

You're looking at my foot, my fat little one. This is just an accident from parachuting. It gives me pain like hell. It makes my life hard. If I had a hammer.

The old woman walked to the corner of the room and bent over. She untied a plastic bag, put the empty can inside, and resealed it.

And this world. This world. He killed himself for this. Men are stupid.

She sat in the chair again, her putrid foot looming large and black for Lea, who stared at it fixedly. The old woman drank more wine and mumbled incomprehensible things, but always with the same rhythm, and eventually Lea fell asleep against the wall, her hands loosening slightly, so that the blanket fell from her warm body, smooth in the dimming light, and the old woman drifted in and out of consciousness, speaking to phantoms, until she was also asleep. Objects became heavy and dark and the walls faded from grey to black until they disappeared altogether and the room became silent and still, with nobody there to witness it.

Lea woke to the old woman's snoring. She pulled the blanket to her chin and sat for a moment listening to the sounds filling the darkness, guttural and wet, until she noticed light filtering through the skylight. She crawled beneath it and lay on her back, wrapped in the blanket, staring up at the wet moons trapped in the layered glass, stars glowing like marbles at the bottom of a puddle. The rain had ceased. The light had always been there, and Lea had always been there, and all of this would continue. Her heart lay comfortably in her chest, where it gurgled and rushed. The light would come again to fill the world, and when it did Lea would return to Christophe and Florian, and even the small children, who were no different than the specks caught in the glass, and had done nothing wrong. She fell asleep between the cool concrete and the wool blanket, humming, and listening to the old woman's throat scrape moons together and apart.

Christophe walked alongside the farmhouse slowly, turning his head from left to right, eyes narrowing, sometimes hunching his shoulders, hands fathoming unseen shapes, creeping lightly, stopping in his tracks, immobile and cocking his head to listen. Marc stood just west of the grass, among the desiccated remains of yesterday's frogs, now bloated with rainwater and half-buried in the wet mud. He watched the old man crane his neck to peek around an unseen object, turn at a right angle, walk in a straight line near the edge of the field, then stop and stare across the courtyard, eyes unfocused, ignoring the siblings altogether. Sabine squatted beside her brother in the wet dirt, holding between two fingers some unrecognizable amphibian organ, hands stained dark with blood and mire.

For Marc the world was quickly becoming a gelatinous landscape composed of non-meted punishment. An empty gale blew through the space Christophe had once occupied. It made the boy nauseous and disoriented. He gnawed his knuckles and watched the old man turn again, drawing a rectangle around the courtyard, lost in his fearful pantomime. Ram a fist through his chest. Crack his face with a log. Crush his arms and legs with a boot. Smear him across a wall. Marc kneaded his swollen nipple and watched the weak creature.

It was after breakfast when Christophe first noticed his wife's absence. She was not in the double bed, which had been carefully made. Not in the shower either, nor using the bathroom, nor reading a book in the living room, nor standing in the kitchen. He called her name, hoping she might emerge from some overlooked room, frowning and telling him to lower his voice, but Christophe knew he had searched the apartment thoroughly. She had not travelled to the store, which had been looted weeks ago.

So Christophe wandered their block, along graffiti-covered walls, staring desperately through smashed-glass storefronts, smelling the long-rotten stench of fruit thrown during the protests. There, the abandoned laundromat where they had washed their clothes, sometimes together, sometimes apart. It was empty and dark. On one of the machines lay an open pizza box, empty as well. He kept searching.

In the penumbra of some ground-floor apartments, a faint sense of human presence. He stared, but was unable discern anything save the occasional rat scratching its way through the detritus, some stray glimmers of glass. Careful to avoid making noise, Christophe leaned around each building to make sure streets were empty before turning the corner. He did not dare wander too far, for fear that if Isabela returned she might find herself locked out. Better to return to the apartment, wait for her there.

Sabine attempted to draw Marc's attention to the grotesque statuette she had been crafting, but her brother was too busy thinking about the old man. Christophe had entered the farmhouse again. Marc left Sabine standing in the courtyard and he walked towards the window. He placed his fingers on the ledge and pulled himself up to peer through it. Inside he could see Christophe sitting in his rocking chair. The old man was reading a book.

A strange restlessness was preventing Christophe from concentrating. He kept looking around the apartment at the furniture, the unchanging furniture, and thinking of Isabela, how her lifeless body would drape over the curb, limbs angled unnaturally, bleeding or already dead, and he cursed himself for agreeing to a temporary exile. Capitulating to her terms, sleeping on that stupid cot in the office. Weakness to give her freedom when she needed protection. Failing to notice her departure in the night. Now the sound of gunshots, explosions in the distance. Paris was no longer safe and perhaps it never would be again. And somehow this fucking idiot wife of his... placing no value on her own life, leaving him to loneliness and sorrow, to death. And perhaps this was her plan all along: edified, a martyr. How small he would seem in comparison.

He put the book down and got on his knees, praying for her health, please lord protect my wife, do not let her die, do not let them find her, protect her today and allow her safe return. Now he prostrated himself, face pressed to the hardwood, and continued his prayer. Save my wife from herself. What have you allowed them to do, and to how many people, how many dead and how many maimed and how many raped, and what kind of god. I am sorry. I am full of fear and I do not know what to do. Please keep her safe, and show me some path forward through my stubborn nature, and deliver me from the bondage of self. I thank you for my beautiful wife and for the fire that inhabits her, and for the decisions she has made, even if I do not understand them. To leave me here alone in this apartment as she wanders this godforsaken city, without a second thought, and tell me god, has she lost her mind. Has she lost her fucking mind.

The mouse groveled on the floor of the farmhouse, skin loose and sagging forward, the fragile notches of its arched spine, the thinning hair, fingers splayed out and trembling on the tile, and the rocking chair immobile behind it. A book lay beside the old man, carelessly cast there when the prayer had pulled him to his knees. Marc hung from the windowsill until his fingers ached and then lowered himself to the ground. There was pain in his wrists and fingers. When it subsided the boy pulled himself up again. Christophe remained prostrate, toes bent back, heels caked in dead skin, brittle and flaking.

Sabine had not moved. She stared at Marc, face absolutely placid, eyes hard and cold. Her brother struggled to keep his face at window level. Sabine walked up behind him quietly and when Marc lowered himself to the ground she kicked him between his spread legs, where she knew the pain would be excruciating.

Lea slept until late morning, and the old woman did not disturb her. Instead she remained in the lawn chair drinking. A deafening quiet filled the room, interrupted only by the sporadic gurgle of flowing drink. The child lay on her back in the center of the room, round white face delineated by soft shadows. She reminded the old woman of a painting she had seen long ago: some nameless cherub compromised by darkness. Of course the child would lose everything, as the old woman had. The grooves in her face and body would deepen until her bones jutted forward in desperation, and then flesh itself would melt away to reveal the underlying structure, hard and white and dead. Even the girl's cunt was a deepening hole where the emptiness had already taken root. The old woman chased these bad thoughts away with the wine. She brought the bottle to her lips until her mind buzzed blankly and her body felt young and light again. When the bottle was finally empty, she reached beneath her chair and produced another.

15.

In that room the two spent several days, although by such cycles neither seemed concerned. Lea spent most of this time resting deeply, her body exuding a stillness that could easily have been mistaken for death. She woke only to feed from the old woman's breast, who by some jumbled agency had resumed lactation: the child refused all other foods anyhow. For a short time, the old woman was calm. She did not tell stories like she had the first night, and they both grew accustomed to the silent presence of the other. The milk was sour to begin with, and chalky, but over this period it grew even more dry and took on the tartness of wine filtered through flesh. This granted Lea comfortable narcosis during her time of respite from the other children.

This went on until the food ran out. The old woman, having no recourse due to her worsening injury, threw herself more fully into drinking. Milk now thickened into grape plasma that no longer contained any nutrition and Lea began to starve as well. With this growing hunger came fear. One night the old woman, now restless, stood over the child, knife in hand, a now-flameless darkness swirling about her polluted mind. Paralyzed by inertia and alcohol, Lea gazed at her with two wet eyes like those of a cornered animal. Finally the old woman collapsed again into her chair, and Lea fell asleep. The next morning, the old woman spoke for the first time in days.

Wake up my fat little one.

Lea did not move. Her eyes darted to and fro beneath their lids.

You listen to your mother now.

The old woman swung her legs to the right, lifted herself, stumbled on her bad foot, straightened out, and walked around the room lighting candles.

Help me with the candles. You help me with these, she said.

Lea did not move. Shades of gold wobbled up the walls and extinguished at the edge of the skylight. The old woman sat cross-legged beside the child and tugged Lea's shoulders until her head was resting on the old woman's lap. One by one she undid the buttons of her own dress, elbows jutting outwards, until it fell around her wrinkled shoulders and the old woman sat bare-chested with the child's cherubic face upturned towards hers. She pressed one dry breast to Lea's mouth and kept it there, her nipple between the child's lips, waiting for her to awaken and begin suckling.

Having sobered considerably, and with a generous headache now, Lea awoke to the old woman smiling down at her. Finding strength she had thought long lost, the child scrambled away from the old woman and crouched naked in the corner of the room, knees pressed to her chin, sniffing her hair and whimpering loudly. The old woman rose. Her brow was knitted and her breasts hung from her opened dress.

You're too good for milk are you, you fat ungrateful beast. I'll wring your little neck. After all I've done for you. After all I've suffered through, to raise you, without so much as a helping hand.

The old woman rushed forward and tripped on the edge of the mattress. Her right hand struck the wall first, and her torso swung inwards, unhalted by her left hand, which refused to drop the bottle, wine spraying in a semi-circle until the old woman's face struck the wall and made a muffled sound against the concrete. The bottle shattered and wine burst onto the mattress and wall and onto the old woman's dress. Lea jumped to her feet and tumbled down the staircase, screams echoing from the upper room, kicking bottles in the darkness as she sprinted towards the door shrieking continuously. She pressed her shoulder to the metal and leaned with all her weight and momentum against the door.

The naked child emerged from the concrete silo, reeling and

holding her hands out to protect herself from the blinding light. All she could see was a white mist in which black dots throbbed. She fell to her knees and twisted around, waiting for the old woman to appear in the doorway and fall upon her, but this did not happen. Soon she could see the dim outline of the towering cylinder, a black shape against the bright white sky, and her bicycle leaning against the side of the building, right where she had left it. She pushed it onto the road and mounted it, water dripping from the seat and down her inner thighs and legs and around her ankles and from her bare feet, and the slope did most of the work, but Lea did not stop pedaling, down a hill, up another, and onwards, naked astride the bicycle, with her hair whipping behind her, clenching her teeth, alternately holding her breath and gasping for air. After several hills the road began to level out, and Lea regained feeling in most of her body. Her throat was dry and wounded. Her arms and legs throbbed with excess blood. She could feel her stomach quivering and empty, calling for nourishment, even if just a morsel.

She turned her head to look at the road behind her, careful to maintain her balance on the bicycle, never to fall, and saw the woman's shape in the distance, black and dense and waving wildly, a black flame leaping over the hill and eddying forward, with two eyes surging from this smoke, opalescent, possessed. Lea snapped her head back and forth. The road ahead still clear. The old woman in pursuit, gaining ground, disappearing behind a hill, reappearing closer than ever. Lea squealed and pedaled desperately, body feverish, glacial, sweating profusely and galvanized by fear. This state of panic lasted for many moments. When finally it began to ease, Lea found herself able to turn her head for longer and observe the apparition more calmly. Slowly the jumbled images became clear in the child's mind. It was only her own black hair, tossed by the wind, and the glistening roadside puddles of rainwater reflecting sunlight.

Lea pushed rigidly forward through her hunger, along the

departementale and towards the farmhouse. She thought of Florian and his long sleep. Brightly in her mind an image appeared, his face very close to hers as she woke him with her mouth pressed to his.

Sunlight around the clouds in brilliant coronas, the shrinking clouds, visible behind the girl's eyelids as great discs of light in the red darkness, the sky a vivid blue, sun loose of the clouds now, warming Lea's skin as she drifted, standing on the pedals, the naked downhill, without fear, without sadness, the cooling wind between her legs, buoyed in movement above the rushing earth.

Marc's pain was like the bottom of a rotten fruit, brown and putrid, with crystalline bristles in a white colony around the edge. The boy pressed his hands to his testicles as it reached the center of the fruit where the pain festered in the stone. Sidewise now and close to the ground, Marc saw naught but pulsating black in the creases of Sabine's tennis shoes, very close now. A rim of mud around the soles, and a long row of stitches, one of them exploded like the tip of a wick. Mud fissuring and detaching in wet chunks as the boy rolled over and groaned.

Sabine looked at the sweat forming on her brother's forehead. His pain was like an unreachable itch beneath Sabine's skin. She had enjoyed watching him collapse, but after a time she grew annoyed by the sound of his groaning and wanted it to stop. Sabine pulled at Marc's arm but found it unyielding, his muscles tensing and relaxing as he massaged his groin. When Marc's pain finally subsided she pulled him to his feet and with one arm wrapped around his waist helped him hobble away from the window. They made their way across the courtyard and towards the comfort of the grain piles where in the darkness he could lie down comfortably.

When Christophe's wife returned, it was on some borrowed bicycle: he could hear the sound of its deflated tires from a street away. The old man dropped his book and leaped across the room, leaning his head out of the apartment window just in time to see her shape disappear into the building. She was wearing a flowing gown of shimmering flesh-toned material, hair loose and brown or black, now behind and beneath him and hopefully free of harm. I will be kind and gentle to her, he thought. It is my fault we are still in the city, and she deserves better than my outrage. Without respect for my wishes or compassion for my anguish, she disappears mid-morning into a collapsing city, and expects me to maintain my cool upon her return. I will maintain my cool, thought the old man, but within reason. He stood in the doorway, listening to her footsteps in the gravelly stairwell, waiting for her to show her treacherous face, that he might calm himself and explain his love in the simplest of terms. I will tell her I love her, thought Christophe.

Lea walked up the stone steps. She had barely passed the threshold of the farmhouse when the slap sent her reeling into the desiccated flowerbed. Christophe emerged from the farmhouse and lifted the child into his arms, soil and loose weeds falling from her naked body as he gripped her tightly.

Where the hell did you go. Have you lost your head. Are you all right. Are you all right. They did not find you. Thank god. Are you all right, he said.

Christophe held his wife and whispered these things into her ear. She remained silent. The old man carried Lea into the farmhouse and cleaned her in the bathtub, noticing bruises on her arms and legs, and a red swelling in her right cheek. There was even a faint purple rim around the bottom of her eye. He dried her with a towel and checked for clean clothes, but found none that were Lea's. And so Christophe wandered into his bedroom and found the white dress she used to wear when they drove out to the Bois de Vincennes and picnicked on the grass, her smiling and pouring him wine, ground uneven below the blanket, glass tipping over and spilling, wife laughing as he scrambled to push it upright, making jokes about the new pattern on the blanket, a modern swedish designer working only in dark red hues. Wine, she meant, wine not blood, did he always have to be so grim. Did she always have to be so foolish. Blankets cost money and money did not grow on trees. Yes teach me about money please Christophe, that always ends well, and he looked at her vicious face and said nothing, and wished he had never spoken to begin with. Christophe left his empty glass on the blanket and looked at her. She sipped her wine and turned to stare at the lake, people drifting along in barques, paddling and chatting and sometimes laughing, and Christophe thought about saying he was sorry, just to get her started again, so she would continue filling the empty air with her words, but he said nothing.

The old man carried the dress back into the bathroom where Lea was sitting on the edge of the tub, her face more swollen than before. She squealed when she saw the dress and Christophe helped her into it and she ran her hands down the bodice, smiling at the old man, but he was staring at something above the child. Eventually his eyes seemed to focus and he patted Lea on the head and gestured for her to join the others outside. He needed some time to think. She walked out of the dining room and made her way slowly up the stairs, on the left side of each step so it wouldn't creak, and into the room where Florian was sleeping.

The old man sat in his rocking chair, aware only of the woven rattan supporting his arms and back. He was alone. Blacker and deeper than before, his eyes dipped elegantly into their sockets like bird's nests in a cliff face, pitted and stained by the autumn showers. Christophe no longer harbored any fear of insanity. His wife was gone. The country had changed. The children were here, gathered. He was born and born again into these familiarities. She didn't do accounting. He was good with numbers. He kept her feet on the ground. She was grateful for this, but sometimes it would be nice to know what he felt, and was that too much to ask? And maybe that's why she left, because he was an empty thing, a structure laboring emptily and without human guidance. Suddenly the old man felt very tired. His hands were locked to the armrests and his knuckles had turned white. And without any of the children watching, Christophe wept.

Marc lay in the wheat, the dry grain infested with flour beetles and rat turds, in the cold room where the concrete walls were humid and rough. He could see the old ladder leading to the crawlspace where the wooden beams and red shingles loomed. The grain hissed and shifted when Marc moved his limbs, reshaping to accommodate his body, and he did this several times before remaining motionless and silent. He could not see Sabine. She had left him in the wheat pile and disappeared. He could not hear anything save the rustling of the fields, which trickled through the open doors with shafts of light from that other world.

Materializing in the silence: a skittering from the crawlspace and the sound of somebody inhaling up there in that crouching darkness.

Rodolphe had been playing quietly with his plastic soldiers. First the boy had heard footsteps, then the movement of grain, and finally a long period of silence. No sound. Bad silence. The soldiers were no longer enjoyable. He had pushed the grenadier forward, trying to imagine the projectile, the way it might scatter the sandbags and dismember an enemy, blowing him into pieces, and the way the pieces would fly everywhere, with all the blood spraying, but Rodolphe didn't care about the stupid plastic soldiers anymore, and they were just toys, and he was scared of this silence, of whatever was lying in the grain pile below. He had swept his trembling hand to gather the soldiers, swatting an infantryman by mistake and watching it skip several times across the concrete, causing him to gasp.

Grain fell from the folds in Marc's jumpsuit as he rose to his feet and walked over to the ladder. He pulled at the wood on each rung, making sure it would not break, securing his feet, left and right, mechanically, left and right, gripping the ladder tightly as he climbed. The boy found himself at the mouth of the crawl-space, his muscles burning, the ache in his testicles gone, and ready to continue his exploration of things, of how they worked and how he might reshape them to his liking.

Rodolphe held his breath and watched the older boy's dark silhouette. If he rushed forward now, like a soldier forward, he might push the enemy out and make him fall over the edge. Like I did with the frogs, thought Rodolphe. Like a real soldier. But instead he held his breath and crouched, palms pressed into the plastic soldiers, hands hurting but no matter, cornered, hoping the older boy would change his mind and leave.

Marc could see the rat's shape. It stood among the turds, breathing scared, which excited Marc, who began salivating rusted metal and moving towards the animal, fists closed and jaw tight. Rodolphe threw the plastic soldiers at Marc and spun around desperately, trying to find a way out, but there was none, and so he put his head down and tried to crawl past Marc, who struck him in the ribs, causing the boy to fall over onto his side. Marc slammed his knee into the rat's belly and watched it curl up breathless, grunting and breathless, and Marc flipped it onto its back, Rodolphe scratching at the older boy's face as Marc spread the animal open, pinning a knee over each arm so it would stop scratching his face, face bleeding onto the younger boy. Marc used a fist to press down on the animal's scrawny neck, fist rolling off the cartilage and flesh and onto the concrete, scraping his knuckles, rocked back and forth by the rat's flailing legs, knees bouncing off his back, then opening his bloody fist and strangling Rodolphe with both hands, holding his windpipe closed until the animal gurgled and slipped one arm, surpris-ingly strong, from beneath Marc's knee, and unzipped the jumpsuit, and clawed the older boy's chest and nipple, with his uncut fingernails full of blood and skin. He gripped Marc's swollen nipple and twisted with his nails. The pain was connected to Marc's testicles and it became unbearable and he was forced to release Rodolphe's neck, which had become smaller and smaller, almost completely quiet, but now Marc fell backwards, twisting his forearms to make Rodolphe release him, and found the younger boy strong, desperately strong, and the two boys tumbled together until Rodolphe loosened his hold, and they fell away from each other and stayed that way for a moment, lying on their backs, Rodolphe gasping thinly and Marc clutching his injured breast.

Marc's blood ran in stripes from the wounds on his upturned face. The other boy kept his eyes on Marc until he felt strong enough to crawl towards the ladder. Marc remained motionless, a string of pain running from his swollen nipple down his spine and into the pit of his testicles. He closed his eyes and saw the shape of Rodolphe's face change with each imagined blow. If he could only find something hard to push into Rodolphe's mouth, breaking teeth, pink gums pouring blood, Rodolphe choking on the blood and teeth, nose breaking, eye pushed into his skull, skull around his eye cracking, nose pulped and pushed into the skull, cheekbones collapsing, lower jaw shattered and pushed into the mouth, nasal cavity collapsing down the center, splitting the face in two, blood rushing to fill the gap, a soup of blood and cartilage and bone, one big crater expanding from the middle, Rodolphe's face unrecognizable with both eyeballs submerged until the breathing stopped and his throat filled with blood and the blood pulled into his windpipe and his heart stopped beating, the perfect silence, skull knocked flatter by the blows, and Marc looked at the peaceful red thing gurgling where Rodolphe's face used to be. When he opened his eyes Rodolphe was gone.

At first Florian did not recognize the sound of Lea's bare feet on the wooden staircase. He assumed his usual position, that of a corpse, and closed his eyes. But as soon as the girl reached the top of the stairs and reached the carpet, Florian recognized the rhythm of her breath, and a series of images came tumbling from the darkness.

In the tree hole where Florian had returned to find the underwear intact, with only the new smell of mold creeping over the others, and a sweet nausea rising within him, until it occupied his throat entirely and felt more like pain than anything else. His body trembled and his breathing grew more erratic as she approached, and he could smell her now, and hear her clearly, and even see the shifting image of her face as if through smoke.

Lea observed Florian. His body was an atrophied thing, with a density and pallor that seemed incapable of movement, like a jagged stone covered in salt scum. He smelled very strongly of urine and sweat. She slipped a hand beneath the sheet and pressed it to his chest where she could feel his ribs beating from the inside. His eyes remained closed, this useless trembling thing, alone in the empty room. She ran her fingers along his clavicle and up his neck and over his chin and across his lips, the fur above, black and rough, and over his nose, feeling his warm breath, the thin and fragile eyelids she dared not touch, his lupine eyebrows, and finishing on the boy's forehead, which she found brimming with the heat of life suspended. She wanted desperately for him to wake and look at her, even if he did so without any kindness in his eyes. Lea decided that she would remain in this room, next to Florian's body, until bedtime came, and perhaps beyond, no matter what Marc or the old man did to her.

She leaned forward and pressed her lips to Florian's, allowing them to stay there, his fermented breath mingling with hers, his nose on her eyelid, cheek to cheek, and again with her lips on his, then touching the different parts of Florian's face. When she pulled back to look at the boy Lea noticed a bump in the covers, where something pressed up, which she dared not touch, fearing she might have caused this new deformation, a form of sickness growing from the boy, feeding on Florian, taking not just his piss but also his blood and sweat, sucking them through the hose and storing them in the milk jug. Eventually Florian would be entirely liquid, and only an empty bed would remain for Lea to kiss. She could not allow it. Lea lifted the sheet and untied the string and removed the hose, which slithered into the milk jug and settled there wet. She looked again where the bump had been, but saw only the boy's limp prick. She had saved Florian.

That evening Christophe fed the children beetroot and cauliflower, sautéed, salted and peppered. He boiled lentils but forgot the seasoning, and the children left them in small piles on the side of their plates until he threatened them and they ate. The old man gathered their dishes and washed them in the sink, noticing red-brown streaks in the running water, and scratches on Marc's face, and bruises around Rodolphe's neck, and Lea's black eye. I cannot run after the children and police them, he thought. I cannot catalogue their wrongs.

Once the children were in bed, Christophe retired to his bedroom. He closed his eyes but found himself unable to sleep. Usually the process was simple. The eyes closed. There was a brief period of drifting. One or two minutes at most. Then he was asleep. But not tonight.

The moon was full and the sky was clear, and through the skylight came a white glow, illuminating the children's faces as they slept. Only Florian lay awake looking at the moon, the feeling of Lea's lips still fresh, and his limbs trembling with nervous energy. He wanted nothing more than to fling himself through a field or climb a tree. Lea had awoken in him the poison of movement and it was driving him mad. He struggled to keep his body still. Safe. Even the moon screamed out until his head was full of noises, wild noises surrounding him, in the mattress, the pillow, and snakes in the milk jug, snakes from the girl's mouth reaching to kiss him with their black lips.

Then across the moon shot a black shape, and the boy's eyes were wide, watching the bat fly from beam to beam, the creature chittering to Florian, who could no longer contain himself, and he sat upright, hands on the mattress, gripping the mattress, legs flung out behind him, until he was on all fours, then pushing with his hind legs to lunge at the bat, to join the bat in its blackness, jumping from bed to bed and stepping on the children's bodies until they woke in a stupor, unable to understand what was happening, even Marc confused, thinking finally the men had returned, and Florian slipping and falling, his thin muscles straining, rising again to jump on the beds, and the bat swooping from beam to beam, terrified, and Florian shrieking and jumping. Christophe coming up the stairs with a belt in his right hand, lit only by the moon, and swinging the belt at the child's legs, to stop this madness, but hitting instead the terrified children, sheets pulled to their chins or over their heads, until they began screaming also, and Florian continued flinging himself from bed to bed, filled with joy and fear, then leaping to the ground, away from the old man, who continued swinging blindly, the boy tumbling down the stairs and through the front door and out into the cold wet air, cutting his hands and feet on the sharp stones, but paying no attention to his pain, no snakes whatsoever, just the smell of the night filling his head with old pleasures, running through the fields and forests, branches whipping his naked body, brambles catching on his arms and legs and marking the flesh, gnashing his teeth and chewing whatever he could, until he had poured everything back into the wilderness, and the wilderness had returned it all, and Florian felt alive, slowing, crawling, limping along, finally finding a soft place among the moss, curling to sleep, peaceful body illuminated by the moon, with the black tattoo of leaf shadow marking his bare flesh.

16.

When Florian awoke into a grey and lifeless day, he could barely remember the night previous. It could have been a fever dream were it not for the many lacerations and bits of thorn still embedded in his skin. Even more incomprehensible to the boy: the profound discomfort he felt lying in the damp leaves and the strength of his yearning for the warmth and comfort of his sickbed.

When the boy attempted to rise, his pain manifested fully. Stiff calves, neck barely able to support his head, thighs cramping unless he locked his knees, even the inside of his feet burned in striations along each toe and into the arches. The boy was a shamble of atrophied muscles trying to keep him afoot. He clung to the trunk of an elm. Slowly he began rubbing himself against the tree bark, forcing his limbs alive, turning his pain into faint warmth, until the cramps receded and his joints loosened and the boy was able to stand without holding the tree, albeit trembling greatly.

Florian squinted through blurred lashes: grey glare of fields, stalktops, sky, a flock of birds turning in one black mass. He grew dizzy immediately.

After crawling with his eyes closed for a long time, Florian cleared the field and found himself on hard flat mud. When it turned rough to the touch, the boy opened his eyes and immediately recognized the ground beneath him. To his right, the path led to the old man and the girl, but also to his father who was waiting patiently for Florian's return so he could drag him by the hair down the front steps, bones clacking on the stone, and out into the courtyard where he would wrap a burlap sack around the boy's head and beat him with a piece of plywood.

No, he turned left instead and continued along the road, limping upright now. To his right soon appeared the rusted husk of a car propped on four cinder blocks, bare axles exposed. Detritus strewn in piles, exploded garbage bags flapping lightly in the breeze. Beyond this disarray lay a house with broken windows, through which Florian could see the spectral contours of dust-covered furniture. The door was wedged slightly off its hinges and he limped towards it.

Lea's left foot squelched into the carpet and her right foot stayed hovering above the black stain. Not two wet feet, please no. Already the left one was slippery and cold, and she pulled it to her nose with both hands. Piss. She used the sheet to wipe it dry, careful to dry between each toe, and lay flat on her belly so she could hang off the bed and take a look, but she already knew what had happened. The blue milk jug had overturned, capsized by the old man in his rush to belt Florian. And now the boy was gone. He had left her alone in the farmhouse with nobody to care for. If Florian returned she would not even look at him. This she swore to herself. Lea stepped from the bed and put both feet down in the piss and walked right through it to find Christophe.

The remaining bits of window-glass were made from the fragmented flesh of some grey animal and they shifted as the boy approached the door. Florian stopped in his tracks to apprehend this new form of life. The stillness of his own pale skin reflected back to him in the dusty glass, frozen there along with his heartbeat. When he moved again so did the images. He repeated this several times until he finally understood that no harm would befall him. The fragments were only the manifold phantoms of light that followed every being, shining back from glass, metal, and water, dimmed only by whatever murky vessel harbored them.

The door swung easy on its hinges but Florian struggled nonetheless to push it open, so weak he had become. The air inside the house was warm and Florian shivered as his body began to adjust, eyes darting around the room to discern the menacing shape of his father, not on the moldy sofa, soft and warm, nor in the doorway to the kitchen, leaning against the jamb, holding a knife, nor crouching somehow beneath the table with its rotten wood and torn plastic tablecloth in red and white checkers. His eyes returned to each place a second time. Nothing. A single red can stood atop the blackened fireplace mantel. Florian had seen this can before. He knew it contained a rough sweetness, if he could only pry it open.

Heavy, it slipped from Florian's grasp and fell to the floor where it rolled several times, collecting ants and flattening dust motes before coming to rest against a table leg. The boy kneeled and reached again for the can, this time careful to hold it tightly as he struggled with the metal tab. He succeeded in wedging a fingernail beneath it and felt the sudden spray of spume as the can exploded open. He drew this new chaos to his lips and with great difficulty sucked from it, spilling a good part down his naked body, so impatient was he to quench his thirst and hunger. When no liquid remained in the can, Florian turned it over in his hands and licked the outside, which tasted of metal and dust. He then discarded the useless vessel and used his hands to wipe the sticky sugar from his body and licked his fingers until they no longer tasted sweet. Finally he pressed his tongue to the floor to lap whatever had spattered there in the dust.

For a long time Florian remained on the floor of the abandoned house, staring at the ceiling as his body awakened. His bones rushed with cool liquid and the boy could feel the bottom of his stomach sliding sweetly towards his chest. Then a swallow darted across the cracked yellow ceiling and disappeared into the ceiling lamp. Florian heard the chirping of baby birds emanating from the concealed nest.

The boy used a chair to climb onto the rickety table, struggling to keep his balance, giddy, and he stood there jumping and flailing his arms, but failing to swat the lamp, until he abandoned this approach and climbed back down to the floor. He picked up the red can and threw it at the nest, but it bounced harmlessly off the sanded glass. Too light. He returned to the garden where he collected stones from the wasted lawn and returned to the house, leaving three stones on the sofa, squinting his eyes and taking aim at the lamp with a fourth. It chipped the side of the glass bowl and the mother bird shot out from the lamp and disappeared through the broken window. Florian could hear the babies chirping wildly now. He missed with the second stone as well and it thumped against the ceiling, leaving a mark and clattering off a commode on its way down.

It was with the third stone that the boy finally succeeded in shattering the lamp. Thick glass rained about him and one of the smaller pieces nicked his shoulder, leaving a shallow wound Florian did not even notice.

It was in death that his wife showed herself completely. Loathsome creature burst open and covered in bruises, at my hands, no, at their hands. Loathe the way your mouth makes noises as you eat, the space you employ for breathing, the things assembled into your lifeless shape. Of course you resisted, of course they were the weak ones, even in death you vanquished us, even as we choked the last bit of life from your eyes. I am a man of the men who did the things that we did to this earth. I am the hand that washes the fist. What god made this man. What god made this coward. Who is the god of vermin, the god of bacteria. Who makes the bloodthirsty and who makes the blood they thirst for. Who makes the endless night in which we forget. Who makes the fruit that rots on the branch. From the tumor to the atom bomb, we will be connecting.

Christophe sat in the car, seatback up, reading something russian translated long ago into french. His eyes were young and they still shone a pale blue as they swept the page from left to right. It reeked of burnt tobacco. She had been smoking again. He would not bring it up. There was no point. She would only lie to him. It was cold inside the car, windows steamed white, winter cityscape a dim blear of faded turquoise, no heating, no motor running, no waste whatsoever if he could avoid it. His wife was inside the unremarkable building, speaking to some civil servant, or waiting without dignity in one of the plastic chairs cemented to a grid, because that is how things are now, Christophe thought, we are beyond redress as a people. So he waited in the car, reading his book and not listening to the radio. Even the classical station had become infected with advertising designed to interest a store owner of his age, a lover of classical music, a man with a wife but no children, somebody the machines had determined to be a devotee of leisure and culture in his free time. They could not have been more wrong. Christophe was no man of leisure, no idle hand, and he did not even think much about music. He owned four compact discs, that was all, and he listened to them once a week at most. Sometimes when he was alone in the car, running errands such as this, he might find himself listening to the classical music station, but this was absent of mind.

Without child, she was, they were, without child absolutely, her womb an empty place. No son, no daughter, not of their blood at least, and of course it was not his wife's fault. But had he known... You would abandon your only family. The one god has provided you. Surely not. Concentrate on your book. But he could not. The smell of cigarettes. The moisture gathering between the windshield and the dashboard. The store closed and for what. So she could retain her tax status as an artist. How much was this costing them every year. And the easel remained folded in the corner of their bedroom, more decoration than instrument. She is busy with the store. That is what matters, he thought.

Then came the squeaking of knuckles wiping moisture from the window in three black strips, a hand knocking at the window for Christophe, somebody's shape wanting to speak to him. Roll down the window. But there was none. Christophe found himself sitting in the burnt-out husk of a vehicle. Only the barest of structures remained, mostly black ash, the gearshift like some black mushroom, the dashboard filled with caverns, his seat a twisted wire of soot, the acrid smell of burned plastic and metal intensifying. As its people, so the city. It had become a daily occurrence now, the burning of cars, their cordoning off and removal, which sometimes took weeks. The removal workers in their suits and masks, and the trucks piled sky-high with blackened debris shifting like toxic sand in their beds. Driving it where.

Christophe's hand pushed through the white car door. It disintegrated into a chalky ash that clung to his skin. The animals had burned his car right under his nose, on the block where he and his wife had been living for years. He stood in the street observing the gutted hood of the old Peugeot like a dormant volcano, a gaping hole of woven ash and shredded parts, turquoise and yellow, black and grey, fused in the fire and utterly unrecognizable. Ash-white cars were parked up the block in both directions, like soap statues crumbling to reveal the twisted viscera of their burnt-out interiors. Christophe wiped his hands on his jeans but the soap refused to fall away. Where was that damned knocking coming from. Like the beating of a drum.

Lea stood fearfully at Christophe's bedroom door, wet feet on the cold tile floor, thinking of the belt, the old woman, the woman in charge of the orphanage, the wild boy, the slap outside the door. All of these she kept suspended in a dim chamber of her mind, the place she used to house disappointments. When finally she heard Christophe's footsteps Lea stepped back and looked up to the part of the door where she expected the old man's face to appear. It appeared a good deal lower.

Where is your mother, Christophe asked her.

Nnnnnnnnnhhh, said Lea, and began to cry.

The old man swept her up into his arms and explained with no emotion in his voice that her mother would surely be somewhere close, all the while looking over the little girl's shoulder at the mechanical carcasses lining the sidewalk. A charred corpse sat in the driver's seat of one of the vehicles. There would be many more lost children if things continued. Surely he could not care for them all. But this girl needed him. She was helpless in a way his wife would never allow herself to be.

Florian found the first baby bird on the linoleum near the sofa, its yellow throat opening and closing, a twitching pulp covered in soft grey down. Carefully he scraped away the bloody shards of glass, wiping his hand on the sofa, and pushed the bird into his mouth, squatting with his elbows propped on his knees and chewing the bones and cartilage and sinew.

The second bird was harder to find. It made no noises, skull crushed in the fall, and was lying a good distance from the lamp, beside a large piece of broken glass near the front door. Florian swallowed it also, eyes aflame, mouth and fingers bloody, using his tongue to clean his fingers of the coppery syrup.

The boy searched for a third corpse but found none. Glass split the soles of his feet as he clambered around the room, pawing the couch cushions, displacing chairs, finally crouching to peer under the furniture. Florian's hunger had abated slightly. It no longer manifested as pain, just a fluid emptiness in his bones, like water running thinly along the interior of a pipe. The birds had been easy prey. Out there in the vastness where the snakes slithered through the grass, there Florian knew he could find more blood, but not before he had exhausted these safe hunting grounds. Florian examined the streaks left on the floor by his own bleeding feet, then looked around the room for some new stimulus. He pushed open the door leading to the master bedroom and crept cautiously inside.

Grey light bled through the sheer cloth of the drawn curtains. The room had once borne life, that much was clear from the ripe musk of sweat and skin and hair sloughed off and smeared into the unmade bed with its twisted sheets and pillows crushed out of shape. Florian pressed his face to these, and their familiar smell conjured up the placental soil of rutting holes, subterrestrial places where the germ of raw life belched forth to purulate in the sunless heat. Rabbit holes, boar dens, mole burrows, the treehole where he had kept Lea's underwear. Again Florian felt his groin flooding with warmth, his prick stiffening uncomfortably against the mattress, until he began with neither shame nor restraint to grind his pelvis against the bed, the room an unmoving cradle for the pale writhing flesh of the boy on the mattress. A metronome of suffocated grunts could be heard and soon Florian's body collapsed inwards and downwards and the boy screamed in terror, thinking his spine was being pulled from him like a worm from the soil.

In the aftermath of his ejaculation, basking in a mixture of dread and pleasure, Florian looked with fascination at the small amount of semen his body had produced unto the mattress. He did not touch it, but instead pushed away from the bed and spun around, only to be faced with another unbelievable sight, a full-length mirror propped in the corner of the bedroom, framed only by plain strips of lacquered pine. It was the first time Florian had seen himself entirely, and he looked first into his vacant eyes, allowing his neck to bend slightly from right to left, examining this full-fleshed phantom standing at the center of the mirror, and understanding in that moment to whom it belonged, that somehow this image was an inseparable part of his being and not just a temporary manifestation. He watched his thin ribs bending inwards and outwards like the yellow throats of baby birds, like flowers at dusk and dawn, in rhythm with the endlessly heaving wilderness, and rickety legs sculpted by grime and shadow, mouth panting, narrow ears throbbing red, mouth crudely painted with bird's blood, stiff black hair like the bristles of a primitive broom, skewed genitals, eyes black and brown, filthy fingernails, swollen belly aquiver.

Me, thought the boy in his abstract language.

And for the first time in his existence Florian experienced his own wretchedness as it appeared through the eyes of others, and a new feeling washed over him. Shame.

The swallow returned to the vacated room, drifting through the broken window and flying in circles along the ceiling's edge. It perched momentarily on what remained of the lamp, head moving in saccades to survey the room, black eyes inscrutable, and then it disappeared again through the broken window.

No she was not beautiful. One of her eyes hung lower than the other and lay deeper in its socket, where due to the shadow of her brow it took on a darker tone of blue. This eye, her left eye, drifted sideways when she was tired or distraught. Her face too was affected by this gravitational pull, jowls hanging from the sides of her thick lips, flat-tipped nose pointing downwards, doughy chin flowing into a smooth and corpulent neck.

Beautiful also the way her skin was singed a dark olive around the eyes and at the edges of her mouth, partly from the exhaustion caused by her many sleepless nights as a teenager, and some as an adult, but mainly because this trait had been passed down to Isabela by her Spanish-Hungarian mother, who in turn received it from her own Spanish mother, all three women prone to the same alternating bouts of irritable languor.

Yes and the way their hair fell dark and wild into the crook of their backs, a camber spotted with birthmarks arranged in mysterious shapes like some mangled alphabet, and leading to their buttocks where a crisscross of cane scars marked each side of the dark bisector, from which black hair escaped in wavelets radiating from the pink center of a soot-covered mountain flower.

No not beautiful with her long thin torso and flattened breasts, long black nipples, thick pubis, hips bulging grotesquely, rippling thighs covered in stretch marks, knees inflexed, a woman both flat-footed and shrimp-toed.

Yes beautiful in the way that she walked, graceful despite her shape, a form of improvised royalty.

The bright bar was filled with a mix of boisterous after-work drinkers, men watching football, barstool casualties hunched over their cloudy glasses of pastis. Isabela wore a low-cut blue dress that padded and swaddled her breasts, above which her smooth clavicles were visible. She sat across the table looking at Christophe, hands folded over his, the man she had learnt to love despite her worst instincts, despite years of abuse at the hands of sadists and addicts and even downright psychopaths. Perhaps he did not arouse in her the same desire as these other men, but with him she suffered less, and Christophe had a way of applying himself between the sheets. She loved him like a painting hung on the wall of her childhood home, Isabela changing fitfully while he remained eternally the same, a steady and reliable witness to her follies, seemingly incapable of treachery. But today Christophe seemed nervous and she watched him struggle to meet her gaze, the sweat on his forehead shining yellow in the side-cast bar light.

Lea sat across the dinner table from Christophe, his cold hands over hers, eyes jumping from thing to thing, the other children eating or staring at him in wonder, confused by this new development. The old man had served them the usual porridge and left his own untouched, drinking nervously from a glass of water and licking his upper lip repeatedly while he observed Lea as the child ate. Christophe had then slowly reached over the table to place his hands on the girl's. She did not know what to make of the old man's vacant stare, and despite having already eaten most of the warm oatmeal, her stomach remained cold and empty. Marc smiled miserably as he watched them from behind his wounds, which had reopened after the thorough scratching he had given them over the course of the morning.

It has been more than three years of shared life, Christophe told Isabela.

Lea looked at Christophe and said nothing. Marc turned to Sabine and touched her arm. She swatted his hand away. They both watched the old man.

Will you marry me, he said to Isabela.

Lea did not answer.

Tears welled in the old man's eyes. All the children had finished eating and they stared at Christophe. Those facing the window could see slow moving clouds behind him in the grey sky, the old man's face dark against that white glare.

I know I do not always express myself well. I know I never do. But I will be a good husband. I promise you, Isabela.

Christophe stroked the child's ring finger.

Do you like it, he asked.

I do, she said. It's a very nice ring. It really is.

He smiled and leaned over the table, kissing Lea lightly on the mouth, his tears wetting the child's face. Everybody in the bar seemed to be staring at them. Christophe rose to stack the dishes, placing the spoons in the uppermost bowl, and carrying everything into the kitchen.

Marc's nipples were now a visible path to his weakness, poking as they did through the cloth of his jumpsuit. He had tried to cut them off with a knife stolen from the kitchen, but the pain was overwhelming and the progress slow, and after a few minutes Marc did not have the courage to continue, his efforts leaving only a crescent-shaped bloodstain on the breast of his jumpsuit. The boy had failed again. There was blood on his face from the scabs picked and eaten, wounds from the younger boy's nails, and now the public shame of these bloated cones of flesh which he decided to cover by folding his arms over his chest. Lea stared pitifully at him from across the spotless dinner table. The old man had shown with his servile tears that he had become the little girl's puppet. Although he was weakening, there remained immense strength in those grey arms. This Marc knew from the swing of Christophe's belt. No matter. Marc would take care of Rodolphe, who would be alone eventually, and this would leave him free to focus on the real threat: the girl and her grey workhorse.

The boy was monstrous. Lea examined the oozing crimson scabs, the bloodshot eyes, the thickening neck, the teeth pink with blood, the way Marc flared his nostrils and tightened the muscles of his forearms, clamping his fists. She wanted the old man to return from the kitchen. She wanted Florian to return to the farmhouse.

Redness was growing inside Marc, spilling through the openings in his body and creating an overpowering stench. Sabine could no longer smell his sweat, and for the first time she felt that he might be changing for the worse. Left to his own devices, he would surely be consumed by whatever force was at work inside him. She would have to reach through her revulsion and restore their bond, without which Marc could not survive. She stood up from the bench and he turned to look at her, eyes momentarily losing their cruelty as she placed her hand on his fist and gestured for him to follow her.

In the dimness of the grain vats Sabine brought herself to Marc like salve to a wound, finding that place of tightness between his legs, the place she had so viciously sought to harm. Feeling her cold hand over his weakness, Marc attempted to resist her, but she gently pushed his hands aside and continued to touch him until the pleasure overwhelmed him and Marc ceased fighting.

Sabine pulled from Marc a pale yellow rivulet carrying in its fluid the snarling mitochondria of the boy's entire existence, and, open-eyed, the boy saw reflected in his ejaculate a series of jagged images, each replayed with agonizing slowness against a backdrop of absolute stillness from which it materialized and into which it disappeared.

Again father chose another boy, an older boy Marc barely knew. He watched father wrap the blindfold around the boy's eyes, his stupid head jerking as father tied the knot. All right, son. Father called the boy son. Now pin the tail on the donkey. Father then placed his open palm on the boy's back and pushed him forward. What the boy held was not even a pin, just a stupid magnet glued to a paper tail, and he staggered with his hand outstretched towards the refrigerator where on a piece of red paper the black outline of a donkey had been drawn. It was my turn, Marc said to the boy, and the look father gave him, one of absolute disgust, cut through Marc so deeply that Marc ran from the scene, up the stairs and into his bedroom, hearing father say to mother, let him go, for god's sake let the boy go. He might learn a lesson. Marc slammed the door and cried into his bedcovers, hoping father or mother might come up the stairs to stroke his hair as he cried and tell him the other children were gone, and Sabine was gone from her crib, and happy birthday. Well boots on the donkey and boots on the boy and boots on mother and boots on father and boots pinning Sabine to the ground.

In its transparent crib the baby was built of bright red stuff. She almost killed your mother, father said, and smiled. Mother rested on the green bed with red string hanging from the red bag and father stood holding Marc and pointing to the baby. Strapped to its face a plastic tube keeping it alive. Part of the baby was pumping up and down. Say hello to Sabine, Marc. Your sister. Marc knew sister meant hurting place, ounce of flesh torn from Marc's own, place where mother and father's eyes would always rest. Sister meant instead. Boots on sister.

Marc watched Sabine tottering along on the grass, not as fast as him, but walking almost running now and laughing. Mother watched from the bench as he chased his sister laughing. Hot smiling day when he pushed Sabine to make her run faster so he could run faster to catch her. She toppled and fell flat with no hands out. There was no joy, no joy at all, the flat face forever flat and Sabine forever gone. Marc looked at the blonde hair and looked at mother and looked at the blonde hair again. He wanted badly to see her face not flat, to see her laugh and smile again. Never would he push her. Never never never. On his knees turning over the sister Marc saw its face still smiling, look up with its green eyes and muddy nose and the blade of grass on its silent forehead. But he had pushed her. Well boots on Marc.

The ejaculate fell onto the wheat in a single strip and like the severed tongue of a frog it collected grain and tumbled downslope. Sabine withdrew her touch and sat watching Marc in the half-light as he ticked like a clock marking the same second again and again. Many times she had seen larger men wilt, but always this had been accompanied by pain. Caught in the grey light canting from the arrow slits in the wall above, the scabs on Marc's chest resembled rake marks revealing clay through a smooth layer of white sand. Sabine's hand traveled over her brother's body to explore these mysterious gashes, but the boy shuddered beneath her touch and twisted his body away, curling into the fetal position. She heard the zipper of his jumpsuit slowly closing and watched Marc's back as he trembled there in the wheat. Again she reached her hand towards the boy and touched the cresting fabric on his left side but Marc jolted back his elbow to knock her away. She did not understand. Her eyes narrowed slightly before she flipped onto her back and let herself slide down the grain pile and left her brother there sobbing quietly.

Florian twisted the bronze key and heard a click inside the armoire. The right door shrieked as the boy pulled it open to reveal a metal bar lined with plastic hangers, bare save one, upon which hung a black blazer. Florian pulled the sleeve and the hanger clattered to the bottom of the armoire. He pressed the blazer to his nose. It smelled of trapped air and Florian let it fall to the floor. Through a crack in the median he could see that the rest of the armoire contained objects, some of them shiny and white. The boy pulled at the left door, but it would not give. He leaned back further, biting his lower lip and grunting, pulling with such force that the wood splintered and the latch burst and Florian was flung backwards onto the floor. He scrambled to his feet to observe the door swinging gently on its hinge, now slowly grinding to a standstill. On the shelves sat folded pants in grey and black and navy blue, and shirts, white and cream, socks in black and brown, and several pairs of black briefs. Florian opened the door completely to reveal a black belt coiled in the corner of the armoire, its stainless-steel buckle shining dully back at him. He looked at it for a moment. He had seen it around Christophe's waist, but also in the old man's hands when he wanted to cause hurt. Florian shivered. Then he began sniffing the items of clothing one by one and discarding them onto the floor in a heap. All of them smelled imprisoned. He would have to make a choice. Continue naked and unprotected or face the stale smell of his former captivity.

The boy pulled a pair of black pants from the heap and put his right foot into the left leg and his left foot into the right leg. Stepping on the cloth, hopping and almost losing his balance, he slowly managed to pull the pants up to his waist, a fair bit of cloth still concealing his feet. He stared down at his hands with his mouth agape and let go of the belt loops. The pants fell to his ankles. Pulling them back up he hobbled towards the armoire and uncoiled the belt, pushing it carefully through the loops, tongue pressed to his upper lip, chin pulled into his neck. He tied the belt into a knot until he was satisfied the pants would not fall again. Then from the heap he removed a white shirt and did not undo its buttons but instead stood with both arms up like a ghostly worm struggling his way into the torso and eventually the sleeves, until his head popped through the collar and he patted the front of the shirt and looked down at himself, then walked over to the mirror and smiled, a skinny boy in oversized formal attire, pants backwards, zipper open to reveal his buttocks, pushing his fingers into the back pockets and delighting in the warmth. He walked back to the armoire and sat on the floor, rolling back his pant legs and pulling several socks onto each foot until they felt bundled and warm. He pulled the blazer over the shirt and looked at himself again in the mirror. Florian climbed onto the bed and rubbed the semen into the sheets with one foot like a dog mock-burying his shit. Then he pulled the covers over himself and began sinking into an all-enveloping heat, in which he felt comfortable and safe, tumbling deeper into a warm darkness disturbed only by his agitated nerves, the cola stimulating his arms and legs and making his heart pound, until the warmth overwhelmed even this last bit of resistance and Florian fell into the first dream of a deep sleep, thin legs jolting up and down beneath the covers as he ran through forests made of cloth, tree branches swaddled in whites and greys and blacks, ground padded with thick blankets, and piles of suitcases arranged like shrubbery along the landscape. Everything was soft beneath his hands and feet, the smell of fermenting cotton filled his aching lungs, and as Florian's muscles weakened he began to fall frequently, but without pain, only to rise again and continue his escape. He could not even hear his own breath through the cottony silence.

17.

A period without incident followed. For a week Christophe was calm and lucid, feeding the children at regular intervals and fulfilling his duties in the garden. Several times he spotted Florian roaming the outskirts of the property dressed like some filth-streaked character from a Beckett play. The old man took to leaving food in a basket, which he hung on the branch of an elm tree he had often observed the boy climbing. The aluminum-wrapped meals disappeared and the basket remained hanging, suggesting to Christophe that the boy was receiving this nourishment in the stead of some wild animal.

Marc's wounds healed and the boy seemed in relatively good spirits save the occasional bout of violence. Sabine remained unreadable, a wide-eyed somnambulist accompanying her brother wherever he went. As for Lea, she often rode her bicycle through the countryside and had recently taken to keeping pets. Christophe would see them hopping and crawling around the house, a few times crushing one accidentally beneath his shoe. Lea marked each death with a solemn and meticulous burial, leaving a rock or stick as a gravestone.

Rodolphe and Gaëlle became de facto leaders for the smaller children who came to favor the safety of the group. Between excursions into the wilderness they remained mostly in the courtyard, mutilating frogs or building miniature villages out of stones and pebbles. Rodolphe entered occasional fits of rage during which he would spend extended time throwing stones against the building's façade. He rarely turned this anger against the others, and the children looked to Gaëlle for consistency and gentleness, qualities Rodolphe did not possess.

All of this Christophe observed with satisfaction. Each day of service to the children was another day spent in penance.

At nightfall, after the children were fed and asleep,

Christophe dressed in dark clothes and slipped out of the farmhouse as silently as possible. The egg whites would have to be culled from Lucien and Joseph, the reluctant old bats. Surely the lord would forgive a theft with such honorable intentions. The moon waxed favorably through a ring of mist and Christophe could see his own breath escaping in light blue wisps as he jogged the road. It was a cold and humid night, and the dew caused the countryside to scintillate in sporadic bursts beneath the moonlight. Christophe turned left on the road and stretched out his hand to stroke a fern frond bowing over the asphalt. His hiking shoes squeaked and the road curved to the right for a long stretch, then to the left. There, outlined against the blue-black landscape, Christophe could see the crudely cemented cinderblocks of the gypsies' house, abandoned long before it was fully built, a burned trailer sitting across from it on the wild lawn. Lucien and Joseph did not have to worry about the thieving no-good gypsies after all. The family was swept off with the same broom as the rest of the countryside. The man, his wife, their two teenage children. All useful. All taken.

As the old man approached the gate he slowed and quieted his footsteps, eyes sweeping the darkness behind the chain-link fence for signs of life. A dog. A stray hen. Perhaps even one of the brothers having a late-night stroll. Unlikely. The dog was long dead, his howls not heard for at least a year, the hens would be in their coop before nightfall, and the brothers were fat and very old, older than Christophe even. They needed their sleep.

Christophe pushed one shoe into the chain link and prepared to hoist himself up. Instead he froze, considering something for a moment before uncoupling himself from the fence. The knob grated as it turned, but the old man could not hear it because the wind was hissing in his ears. Christophe pulled the gate open and slipped inside.

The courtyard was bare and empty. The two-story house cast a long shadow and its black windows reflected no moonlight. To its left stood a chicken coop shoddily cobbled from rough planks, a small padlock securing the door. Christophe ran his fingers over the latch and wiped the flaking rust onto his pants. The nails were loose in the rotten wood. From his coat he removed a screwdriver and wedged it between the latch and the door, using it as a lever to separate them. It gave easily and he did not have to struggle. He entered the coop.

Christophe could hear the hens scuffling in the darkness. He produced a plastic lighter from his pocket and struck the flint. Seven birds lined the roost. Two were asleep. The rest watched the old man with their black eyes. They smelled intensely of rotten straw and bird shit. Christophe shushed them as he had seen Lucien and Joseph do, but they did not seem agitated. The old man examined the nesting boxes and found thirteen eggs in the plastic containers. He took eight, slipping them carefully into a plastic bag hanging from his wrist. The hens said nothing. Christophe closed the door behind him and pushed the latch nails back into the wood. They were looser than before, but the brothers would probably not notice. He crept back across the courtyard towards the gate, making sure to close it behind him.

A dull joy rose in the old man's breast as he walked towards the farmhouse. He did not notice the moon as the clouds drifted from it, nor did he reach out to touch any plants. He walked upright and absorbed in thought, a black shape on the grey road.

Tonight Christophe did not feel old. His bones did not ache in the usual manner, and instead of sleeping he rolled up a piece of scrap paper and used it to light the oven. Because it consumed a great amount of gas, the old man had not used the oven in years, but tonight he would make an exception. Meringue was by definition a wasteful and frivolous thing. He lit two candles so that he might see his workspace and cracked four eggs, passing the yolks back and forth in their shells, and letting the whites drip into a bowl. The yolks he kept separately for tomorrow's soup.

Christophe beat the egg whites with trembling arms, driving

the whisk in tight circles until the mixture looked like sea foam. As he walked towards the pantry Christophe heard the buzz of a fly and turned to see its enormous shape projected onto the wall, black against the orange light. He watched it fall into the bowl and go silent. In the pantry he felt around in the darkness and carried various paper containers into the light until he found the caster sugar. He walked back over to his workspace and set the sugar next to the bowl. He could see a small hole in the mixture where the fly had entered it.

Christophe pushed his finger into the hole and attempted to scoop the insect out, feeling instead the vibrations carried through the hollow muck, the relentless beating of the fly's wings in the foamy darkness as it struggled to remain alive. In that moment he glimpsed the tremendous solitude of death and the old man cried out, his shadow billowing in the flickering candle-light as he staggered backwards and collapsed against the sofa. Slowly the old man's head dipped until his chin was resting against his breast and his face was lost in shadow. He stayed that way until the candles had halved.

18.

Florian spent the entire winter in his new home. He masturbated until his foreskin was numb and his fingers were numb and his ejaculate grew clear and then barely came at all. With each climax his pleasure became more skeletal and exquisite. The boy's testicles were made of hard, frostbitten dirt, and they slowed Florian with the raw weight of their protest. Only sleep could silence them. Each night the boy wrapped himself in the covers and felt his bones and muscles growing painfully as he listened to the wind roaring in the broken windows. At dawn he rearranged his clothes and ventured half-heartedly through the front door.

His first steps were always agony. He took them eyes closed and trembling, following the same path through the backyard until his heart settled into a middling discomfort and his eyelids parted to allow for sight. There was so much of everything. Every leaf was made of smaller leaves, and each of those were made of leaves smaller still, and this continued until the mind could not comprehend what any of it meant. The boy no longer cared what could be found beneath a stone, or what might lie at the bottom of a puddle. When a snake dies, it deflates and lies limp on the ground until it evokes nothing but the exhausted memory of past fear. Florian was no longer afraid of the wilderness, nor did it beckon him. It was a burdensome and intricate thing. It did nothing but explain itself again and again. Only ejaculation had the power to briefly lift the veil of that grey winter.

But the girl remained. She did not make Florian blind with pleasure, but smoldered instead beneath the surface of his unease. Sometimes when he journeyed to the farmhouse to retrieve food from the basket he would find her riding her bicycle around the courtyard or sitting by the pond, lost in some reverie. Her presence never failed to stir pain. Florian felt the heartache of standing in the antechamber of all creation, its manifold sights and sounds carrying faintly through an opaque membrane he dared not touch. Only the knowledge of Lea's existence gave Florian the strength to continue living. Each day before rising, he lay on the bed with his eyes closed and conjured her smell. It supplied him with some semblance of resolve.

Over the course of his daily wanderings, Florian discovered a nearby building, long and windowless and flanked by bushes and trees. Its walls were beige and its roof was grey and its single door was made of shiny white plastic. The exterior was bare and monolithic and conjured no thoughts. This calmed Florian greatly.

One day, after a few hours of staring at the building in silent worship, the boy's toes had gone numb from the cold. The sun was disappearing behind the building and a glacial wind began strafing the countryside. For the first time, Florian walked towards the building and opened the door. Once inside, the boy's eyes were drawn to the natural light coming through a long strip of transparent plastic embedded in the metal ceiling. It gave the room a grey and shadowy look. A row of fluorescent tube lamps hung on each side of the strip. They were unlit. The room was entirely covered in tile and Florian was mesmerized by this rigid geometry. Faint boot marks led through several rows of white-grey racks containing plastic tubs. Each of these was lined with cheesecloth stained by the black and turquoise arabesques of long-dead mold colonies. Only a faint smell of decomposition remained, and it seemed to be coming from behind a doorway blocked by a transparent plastic curtain. Its filthy strips reflected the boy in blurred sections. He probed these with his fingers, finding them malleable. They crackled as he pushed them apart.

The boy found himself in a long, dark hallway, at the end of which Florian could see another set of curtains through which shone a sullied light. A black shape lay on the ground near that doorway. Florian stood observing it for a time, but it did not move. A rivulet of bile trickled down the back of the boy's throat. He could feel his heart beating in his ears. Florian advanced towards the shape, the hallway narrowing and blackening until he was close enough to see.

It was one of his own kind, wearing a blue dress with a white apron, both stained, and a pair of dark green rubber boots, lying on her side, head forward, wrists inward and pressed together, legs scattered apart. Not legs exactly, nor wrists, but only a skeleton wrapped in desiccated grey-black flesh and burst open in parts, eyes like black boreholes leading into the skull. Here the smell was strong, disgusting even, but Florian was not scared. He knew this was only the shell of a creature long disappeared. His heart beating more steadily now, the boy pushed through the curtains.

The room was split into sections by a short chain-link fence. Against the right wall stood a large structure with tubes hanging from the ceiling and into steel scaffolding. It was connected to a fenced-off corridor leading into the main part of the room, a large enclosure filled with black things piled one upon the other: ribs, vertebrae, femurs, tibias, skulls, fur, leathery black flesh, horns, hooves, and plastic tags in blue and yellow. All of these things springing from one another as if they were part of some greater molten organism filling the entire room. In the corridor beneath the scaffolding Florian could see individual corpses laying on the hardened filth, their dried udders collapsed into the black nozzles of milking tubes. Just as the old man had gathered Florian's urine, this machine had stripped the goats of their life.

This was not death as he had known it in the wild. It was a new death binding the putrid and burned smells of metal, plastic, piss, shit, ash, wood, flesh, and vomit. Dull wide smells and sharp acrid smells reached Florian's nose inseparable.

When he finally exited the building Florian did not even notice how cold the air had become. The hair on his arms and legs raised and his skin turned to gooseflesh and his muscles hardened and his testes rose towards his navel and his prick shriveled into a nub. Beneath the pale dusk Florian shuffled along the road towards the farmhouse, scraping his bare toes on the asphalt.

The old man called the children to dinner and Marc ate his portion faster than Sabine and walked out into the courtyard, away from the weight of his sister's silence. Even as he watched the fields sway and the rocks jut from the dirt and the wind blow steadily across the courtyard, the boy's solitude was not peaceful. She had touched Marc in a cold and dead way. He made his way to the pond.

It was a crooked thing, rutty banks overrun by goosefoot and heather. From this tangle of weeds grew lopsided elms and meandering beeches and a single weeping willow on the north-ernmost bank. From the shallow waters on the pond's edge came flowerless daffodils and dead reeds growing in tight bunches. It was on the path along the eastern bank that Marc noticed Florian floating along in his baggy clothes like an empty thing, and he did not know what to make of him. Marc hid behind a tree and observed the other boy.

When Florian reached the edge of the pond he leaned over the water to watch the shapes change, as he had often done. Beneath the surface something swished, stirring the mud, and the dying light caused Florian to see only the faint outline of a face rippling on the surface. My face, he thought. Wind blew the grass back and forth around his bare feet. They were wet with dew and very cold.

The round shapes purled in tones of grey and green and brown until Florian was unaware of his surroundings and found himself thinking again about the place of shines. At the bottom of the muddy water, there everything existed as it had before the snake, before the winter, before the building filled with death like a lamp full of flies. And there the girl would be waiting for him with her glowing ruddy cheeks and stubby teeth, the way her lips were wet and warm, the smell of her hair and her clothes and her underwear, the way she might chew her nails or toenails like a distracted dog and make noises like a bird. All these tangible things transmuted into diamond-light spinning into and out of itself. Yes, to put an end to his suffering, Florian had only to release his body from the shackles of posture and let it topple forward into the water.

Marc watched Florian sway back and forth at the edge of the pond. The boy was in a trance. Back and forth he swayed with his eyes closed, each time more precariously, until finally he tipped forward and fell from sight.

It was curiosity that led Marc to the pond, but this alone could not account for his speed. He sprinted towards the mound from which Florian had vanished and looked into the water and saw beneath the surface a mass of clothes billowing like a jellyfish midst the swirling mud.

Marc leapt from the bank, cheeks blown out, eyes furious, body going rigid as it struck the water and was swallowed by the cold darkness. The boy's feet plunged straight through the pond-bottom and Marc was forced to thrash about until they came unstuck from the thick mire. His lungs seized violently and he swam in a panic until his arm struck Florian, a hard and unmoving thing, perhaps dead already, or perhaps never having contained life, so dead did he feel when Marc gripped his wrist. He attempted to pull Florian towards the embankment but could not even keep himself afloat, and Marc's mouth and nose filled with water until he was certain he would drown, but he did not accept this certainty, and so he fought with all his strength against the cold water and did not loosen his grip on Florian's wrist. He pushed at the mud for leverage but found none. After a long struggle Marc found himself among the reeds, arm wrapped around Florian's neck, grunting and sputtering, bending and crushing the daffodil stalks, pulling at them desperately and finding in the sum of their roots the solidity required.

Soon the boys were in shallow water and Marc was able to stand with his head above the waterline. His legs labored through the mire and slowly he dragged Florian to the edge of the pond where he left him lying against a thick bunch of reeds as he pulled himself onto the bank. From there he leaned down and gripped Florian's wrists and attempted to pull the boy out of the water. Marc dug his feet into the grass and struggled to find leverage. He ground his teeth, biting both sides of his tongue until he tasted blood. After several moments of effort, he succeeded in dragging Florian's torso onto the bank, and then his legs, and as he did so the boy's head lifted, and Florian's face was covered in mud, and two eyes opened to look at Marc, white and bloodshot around the dark pupils, and Florian lunged forward with his mouth open and sunk his teeth into the other boy's hand. Marc screamed and kicked but Florian refused to loosen his jaw and finally Marc struck his face, fist plunging through the sludge and connecting with a nose bone. Florian fell backwards onto the hard ground, where he gasped and writhed and vomited brown water.

Marc looked at his hand. Mud and blood mixed in the gashes left by Florian's teeth, and this pink and brown liquid streamed from Marc's hand and was swallowed by the grass. He walked across the courtyard and towards the farmhouse, where he found Christophe standing in the doorway, looking at him.

You went and put yourself in the pond, said the old man.

Marc looked at him and said nothing.

Do not enter the house. Do not move. Stand right where you are.

The boy did as he was told. There was anger in the old man's voice and Marc knew to be afraid of the belt. He watched the old man walk across the courtyard and pick Florian up by the collar and drag him snarling and snapping towards the farmhouse. Florian attempted to bite Christophe, and when he did, the old man stopped walking and slapped the boy across the face, and

Florian stopped struggling and let himself be dragged. Christophe dropped Florian's limp body next to Marc.

Both of you stand up, he said.

Marc was already standing and Florian rose uncertainly to his feet. They were dripping with mud and Marc's hand was bleeding. Both looked at the old man and said nothing. Christophe walked along the farmhouse and unraveled the hose and turned it on. A cold hard jet of water shot forth from the nozzle. First he used it to wash his hands of mud. Then he walked back towards the boys, keeping the hose pointed at the wall of the farmhouse, against which the water exploded into a rough mist.

Step away from the house, he said.

The boys did so. He sprayed them with cold water and they grimaced and blinked and attempted to protect their bodies with their hands. The jet stayed one step ahead of them, and the old man barked at the boys to turn around, keep turning you little idiots. Then he pointed the hose downwards and watched the two boys dripping in the courtyard, and told them again to turn until he was satisfied.

Take your clothes off, he said.

Marc and Florian stripped slowly until they stood naked and shivering in the courtyard, illuminated by the pale yellow moon, its craters plainly visible against the dark blue sky. Both of them were streaked with mud in strange patterns and Florian's long hair covered his eyes. They are going through changes, thought the old man. They are barely boys any longer.

Why in god's name would you play in the pond when you know it to be full of mud, said the old man.

He flicked his wrist and the jet of water lifted, striking Florian in the face and the boy lifted his hands instinctively but Christophe whipped down the jet so that it struck Florian's belly, which caused the boy to lower his hands again, allowing the old man to finish his work.

Turn, he said.

And Florian did. This will teach the boy to ruin perfectly good clothes, thought Christophe. Do I remember giving him those clothes. That white shirt and those loose pants and that belt. I do not. Surely I do. But I do not. No matter, they were his clothes, and he ruined them in the pond, and now he is being punished.

When Christophe had finished with Florian he turned the jet to Marc. This boy's behavior is surprising, thought the old man. I do not know him to be a fool. He is sometimes brutal, and often cruel, but rarely foolish. Look at him shivering with his teeth clenched and his muscles braced. He turns like a soldier when I instruct him to do so.

When he could see no mud on their naked bodies Christophe turned the hose to the wall and walked alongside the farmhouse again. He closed the tap and coiled the hose. Then he turned to make sure the boys had not moved. Neither had. Florian was hunched over, arms folded across his chest, hands tucked into his armpits. His teeth chattered loudly and his hair had fallen in front of his eyes again. Marc also had his arms folded, but his teeth did not chatter. His jaw was clenched so tightly that its muscles twitched. He stood straight and stared defiantly at Christophe. But he would never dare, thought the old man. Still his eyes are indomitable.

Do not move, the old man said, and disappeared into the farmhouse.

Marc's hand ached terribly but the boy did not look at it. His blood dripped onto the dirt, forming there a shapeless stain only slightly darker than that of the water. It could have been the shadow of a fly cast from the windowpane. Florian looked at his own feet, the oversized articulations and the black toenails grown long through the winter. Then he looked at Marc. Florian could smell the blood. It seeped from the hand responsible for pulling him back into the world.

Christophe reappeared in the doorway with two clean towels. He threw one over his shoulder and wrapped the other around

Florian, who clutched the fabric to his chest with skeletal hands. Christophe looked at him in the eyes and held the boy's jaw between fingers and thumb until Florian's teeth stopped clacking. Then he wrapped the second towel around Marc.

Do not let them touch the ground, he said.

Christophe fetched a rag from under the sink in the kitchen, and laid it carefully down across the bottom step.

You first.

The boy said nothing but stepped forward onto the rag. Christophe gripped Florian's left ankle and lifted the boy's foot, using the rag to wipe the mud from beneath it as Florian held onto the old man's shoulder for balance. Christophe then pulled the rag from under Florian's left foot and made him stand on the cold dry stone while he cleaned the boy's right foot. Once this had been accomplished he ushered Florian into the farmhouse. The old man then flipped the rag and repeated the same actions for Marc, who also held the old man's shoulder for balance. When he was finished Christophe rose and pressed his hand to Marc's naked back and gently pushed him up the remaining steps and into the farmhouse, where from the dining room the boy could see the other children gathered in the kitchen. Lea had carried a blanket down the stairs and wrapped Florian in it. The girl was sitting on the sofa holding him in her arms. She smiled and wept. The boy's eyes were closed. The others stood around them keeping vigil in the dim orange candlelight.

19.

With the first rays of spring Christophe carried a wooden chair out into the courtyard and sat facing westward, enjoying the sunlight on his skin. The wind blew stray cumulus across the sky, none of which obscured the sun, and between gusts, when the sun beat continuously, Christophe warmed to the point of comfort. He wore no shoes or socks and was dressed in filthy grey slacks and a stained white undershirt. His stomach had grown round from inactivity. Christophe's skin was more flaccid than before and jowls hung from his once sturdy face. No matter. He held his back straight, and beneath the drooping exterior he was made of steel. She would not bend him. She would not break him. It had been a week now since she had disappeared, and Christophe had almost called off the wedding despite the flimsy note she had left behind.

I WILL BE THERE, the note said, BUT I HAVE SOME THINGS TO TAKE CARE OF FIRST. I HOPE YOU UNDERSTAND.

So she would open her legs one last time for the world before she committed to mediocrity. Surely among her squatting friends in the suburbs she would find a mattress to lie on. There she would find bottomless, irresponsible pleasure.

When the phone did ring it was always the florist, the owner of the pavilion du lac, or some other commercial representative preoccupied with logistics or payment. Isabela had few friends, having traveled so often and given so many people a piece of her mind, and he did not have much of a social life either, finding the presence of others distracting and preferring the straightforward structures of work, literature, and museums. The wedding would be a low-key affair held in the Buttes-Chaumont. Not many guests. Some fellow Belleville storeowners. An estranged uncle. No parents, long dead. The joining of two only children.

At the edge of the courtyard Lea held Florian's hand as they watched the old man speak to himself. His voice rose and fell. He nodded. Then his eyes closed and his jaw hung open and Christophe turned his grey face to the sky.

Lea squeezed Florian's hand and the boy looked up at her. She made him understand what she wished them to do. He nodded. Recently the old man had taken to seasoning meals with sugar instead of salt, or cooking vegetables until they grew black and limp. Sometimes he even forgot to serve meals altogether and when the children gathered to be fed at the appropriate time, the old man reacted with anger. And so Lea had taken it upon herself to visit the garden and gather a small batch of vegetables every so often, distributing these in a relatively even manner among the children.

When Florian and Lea reached the northernmost edge of the farmhouse they turned to look at Christophe one last time. His eyes remained closed. They walked around the farmhouse and into the garden, where the gnarled apple trees stood in uneven rows, branches lined with young flowers. Florian did not like spending time in the garden, no matter how many times Lea brought him there without consequence. He still remembered the beatings of his early days on the farm, before he had learned the old man's rules. The boy crawled the periphery of the garden while Lea performed her best imitation of Christophe's daily inspection, bending leaves between her thumb and forefinger, staring at blossoms, and smelling certain plants.

Florian was a restless and gangly creature now. He had lost the grace of his pre-pubescent years and his body was long and thin, the ankles and wrists and knees disproportionately large, a giant head lolling back and forth like an untethered balloon. He had real difficulty staying balanced, and often knocked his shoulders against walls or trees, but used them as springboards to resume his enthusiastic stride. His nature was gentler, too, and he often smiled, but it was a sad and diffuse smile.

Something about that day did not feel conducive to food

collection. Lea followed Florian into the field where there was no shade. There he wrapped his arms around her and pulled her down into the weeds. Soon she was hysterical with laughter and began rubbing the top of her head on the boy's chest and stomach, which caused Florian to roar with laughter and push her away. She squealed and continued to throw herself at him headfirst, and soon they were both in a state of nervous exhilaration bordering on mania. Florian's crooked grin floated between the stalks and his face was pink and flushed, and Lea chased him through the grass until she grew tired from the heat and lay down to rest.

When Florian found her she was lying on her stomach and he rushed forward and fell to his knees and tickled her ribs but she squirmed in disapproval and he stopped. Her dress was hiked about her midriff and he could see her white underwear stained in little overlapping rings of dried excreta. Florian put one sweaty palm on each side of Lea's underwear and she said nothing. Then he put his palms on the small of her back, where sweat had gathered in a pool, and he kept them there for a while, warm and wet. Finally Florian pulled down Lea's underwear so that her buttocks were exposed.

He kneeled over the girl, transfixed by these two glistening moons, her pores like tiny reflective pools scattered across these white surfaces. The boy placed one palm on each side of the narrow canyon. His hands trembled and he was filled with a strange joy. Lea was silent and her brown hair spread unevenly to each side of her nape among the dust and broken stalks. They remained that way for a long time, the boy perfectly suspended above these moons like the black universe itself pressed to their flawed and glimmering surfaces. Eventually the boy saw reflected in these two mirrors his own awful image, split-eyed and leering, and there was nothing bizarre about it. He closed his eyes and felt the heat of Lea's flesh beneath his fingers, at once a part of him and not, and he was happy for the first time in years.

Marc turned to Sabine to see whether she was also watching Florian. She was. The boy's head appeared above the weeds, eyes closed, long black hair moving with the breeze. Marc could not see what was happening in the grass below, but he had seen the two enter the garden and remain there for a period. It was not the first time Marc had seen such a thing. Perhaps the old man no longer held authority there. When the forests are dry, Marc thought, we will gather food of our own from the garden, real food, and use it to tend to our family. They will no longer spit any part of our meals onto the ground, and they will not cry. Instead our children will love us and look to us for protection and do whatever we tell them to. I will be the father, and she will be the mother. Then everything will be in order once more. As long as the old man does not interfere.

Marc left the shade of the mirabelle tree and walked towards the courtyard to see if Christophe could still be found planted on his chair in the courtyard. Sabine stayed two paces behind Marc and trod lightly.

Isabela's uncle and his wife were the first to arrive, him with the discomfited dignity of a poor man wearing a suit to a stranger's wedding, and her looking absolutely disoriented as she followed him. A waiter led them into the back room and Christophe greeted them and showed them to their seats near the head of the long wooden table. The uncle was stout, built of tough material, maintaining a serious look. His wife was an unassuming creature, and she remained silent unless spoken to. They sat facing each other across the wide table, and after a few attempts at small talk Christophe left them alone and walked over to a mirror, where he adjusted his tie. Isabela had returned the night before, looking exactly as she had before her disappearance. No trace of strange hands. Carrying only the blue sports bag and her usual black leather purse, one of the only physical remnants of her life before Christophe. She did not wear an apologetic look but instead kept her chin thrust forward and acted as if the whole episode was something they had planned together. As if she had accomplished her duty by disappearing during the weeks leading up to the wedding. In his belly Christophe could find nothing but the dregs of his previous anger.

The siblings sat cross-legged in the dirt of the courtyard, observing the old man as he wandered back and forth across the grass and spoke to himself, avoiding unseen objects and holding the sapling with one hand as he stared out over the fields. Christophe seemed distraught and Marc thought it best to stay with Sabine where the old man had forced them to sit.

Gaëlle led Rodolphe and the others along the hedgerow. They had spent the day climbing trees and chasing each other through the forest. They had killed each other with rifle-sticks and sword-sticks and spent a long time arguing over who was dead and who was alive. The children trusted Gaëlle to give the final verdict on such matters. She was more trustworthy than Rodolphe. Again today the boy had refused to accept his own death, even though the children had all seen his killer pierce Rodolphe's chest with a sword. When Gaëlle would not change her decision, Rodolphe sat on a log and refused to play, even though the smaller children, idiots that they were, continued to shoot and stab his unresponsive body. He kept his arms folded across his chest and pretended not to notice until they left him alone. As the others resumed their game Rodolphe forced his eyes to look uninterested and his face to appear blank. He wanted very badly to join them again, and they probably would have welcomed him back, but now it was too late. Rodolphe hated being in this situation, but he could not change the way he was. He wanted the children to beg him to participate. He would slap away their hands and they would insist and finally he would join them and everybody would cheer. He wanted to be the king and the leader and the best soldier. But instead he was alone with his rotten thoughts and he loathed himself and everybody else. But Gaëlle always managed to coax him back into the game. She was the better leader and he knew it. So did the others. But he did not hate her.

Gaëlle woke Rodolphe from his reverie and pointed towards the courtyard, visible now between the trees. Christophe was turned towards the arriving group. It was too late to turn back. The old man stood in front of an empty chair at the center of the courtyard. Sabine and Marc were sitting in front of him on the ground. Gaëlle waved the children onwards and they soon reached the end of the hedgerow and turned onto the path. Marc and Sabine were watching them now. Rodolphe searched the older boy's face but there was no particular expression there. The old man smiled as he walked towards the incoming group.

Now the storeowners had arrived. Unlike Isabela's relatives, Christophe knew how to speak to them. They had the neighborhood in common. Even if Christophe did not always participate in the conversations, he still enjoyed hearing about rotten stock, belated deliveries, and other work-related business. What he liked most about these men and women is that they were not in the habit of gossiping. When they discussed situations, they usually stuck to quantifiable facts. They would not, for example, refer to someone as a deadbeat. Instead they might state the size of that person's debts and how many weeks it had been since their last payment. Even when they passed judgment, it was bereft of malice. One of them might say, for example, so and so is not in the habit of paying his tab at the brasserie, and the others would nod solemnly. This Christophe admired. He hated people whose eyes would dance with glee as they described the local drunkards or told the story of a domestic row they had overheard a few nights prior. This only spelled discord for the neighborhood, which already had its fair share of problems. People were being forced to sell their storefronts and move elsewhere. Communal gardens were under threat of being shut down. Pickpockets roamed the boulevard stealing from café tables. On one side were the damn sharks, and on the other the petty thieves. Both were bad for business.

But Belleville would survive them all. Honest work endured, and these were honest workers. There was Monsieur Karam from Les Délices du Liban. His rectangular glasses were filthy as usual and he carried a bag of purple olives. Walking alongside him was the young Monsieur Chen from Chen Fruits & Légumes. He wore a fitted vest over a white shirt. His wife was with him. She was an older chinese woman who did not speak any french and seemed to scowl at Christophe. He knew about their marital quarrels and hoped she would not cause a scene today. Behind them walked Madame Delacour from the boulangerie at the corner of Simon Bolivar. She had brought her eldest son Jacques, a heavy-set boy with ruddy cheeks. He looked uncomfortable in an old-fashioned suit, no doubt his father's. Christophe had attended the man's funeral not two years ago. He greeted them with a kiss on each cheek and shook Jacques' hand. The boy's hand was limp and sweaty. His pupils were larger than most. Christophe turned back towards the pavilion and his dead neighborhood followed him.

Christophe took his seat at the head of the table. Nobody spoke. They looked exhausted. All of these working people had a long week behind and a long week ahead. This is my wedding, but for them it is just another weekend function, Christophe thought. They are dressed in rags. Look at their tired faces. Look at their...

Christophe rose from the table and walked back to the doorway, peering into the main room. It was empty. Closed to the public. Very little light made it through the long glass panes. The trees had moved closer to the pavilion and they stood blocking his view of the path on which Isabela would arrive. But they were not trees. They were people pressed to the windows, breathing little jets of fog, the children below with their eyes wide, the adults hovering above, turning to one another and discussing some detail of the interior. Why have they not opened this area to the public. These people only want to eat their Saturday meal, thought Christophe. Somebody should open the place. He wandered from room to room but could find no waiter. His guests sat silently at the table. They watched him come and go. When he returned to the main room there were more people pressed to the windows. Some of the teenagers were standing in tightly bound groups and pulling apart each other's clothes. Younger children gnawed at their bleeding legs, mouths open and screaming, but silent through the double-glazed windows. The adults could not see these goings-on. Only Christophe stood witness. How was Isabela to pass through this crowd. He could not think of any solution. He called out to the waiters, to the owner.

Lea's body went cold when she heard Christophe yelling. Marc is attacking the old man, she thought. He is killing the old man. Florian wanted to continue playing but Lea opened her outstretched palm and stopped the boy in his tracks. He tried to understand the source of her distress by observing the girl's face. Her head was tilted back and her eyes fixed the sky with empty intent. She tucked her hair behind her ears to better listen. When the sounds came again, Lea pressed her hair to her nose, breathed deeply, and looked at Florian. He too could hear the old man's cries. With her spare hand Lea reached for Florian's. Together they began walking cautiously towards the farmhouse, crouching low among the wheat stalks.

Of course the owner never showed, nor did his waiters. They had failed miserably at the simple task allotted them. He would remember to raise the matter when it came time to pay the bill. After a while Christophe ceased calling for the staff. Anyways it mattered little; the crowds had begun thinning around the pavilion. They went elsewhere for their Saturday meal, taking their teenagers and children and prams with them. Some were bloody, missing pant legs, some half of their faces, some being wheeled on stretchers, some wearing burned clothes or mutilated even.

Already Christophe felt calmer. He returned to his guests. A few were standing impatiently. They scrambled to sit down as they saw Christophe approach. Some had even swapped seats. He would allow this. There was no point insisting. Already they wore bitter and confused expressions.

They do not trust me to provide a meal after the ceremony, he thought. But a meal has been promised and a meal will be provided. They do not need to worry.

Of course it all hinged on the staff, but Christophe felt confident they would reappear in time for the meal. It was the ceremony that worried Christophe. He should have insisted on the church. Saint Jean-Baptiste de Belleville would have been a more appropriate setting.

That is the look on their faces, he thought.

What wretched man cannot convince his future wife to exchange vows in the neighborhood church?

During her absence the store has suffered.

Children call him Stone-face because he never smiles.

Yes he is organized, but does he enjoy his life?

Look at him scowl as he paces from room to room.

Is that the face of a man on his wedding day?

Christophe could no longer look at his guests. He walked into the main room and found the park mostly empty. Stray groups of late picnickers.

When Isabela appeared, it was with the priest at her side. They stood for a moment next to a large maidenhead tree, its green branches overlapping like wave trains in a turbulent sea. The two figures were small in its shadow, her in a simple white gown, him in a black cassock. Seeing her like this from a distance, Christophe was overwhelmed with pity. She was fierce and restless and would always live alone. He could marry her, yes, and even share a home with Isabela, but this meant nothing. Christophe watched her lift the hem of her dress to walk through the grass. She was wearing sneakers. The priest spoke to her, but

Christophe could not hear them through the silence of the closed pavilion.

The old man's smile looked strained. There was no blood on his face, and none on his shirt or pants. He walked in his usual way. It seemed no harm had come to him. But his eyes were vacant in that now familiar way, and as Lea looked past him at the other children sitting on the ground, she felt the bottom of her belly turn to vinegar. Christophe shook Florian's hand nervously and held Lea's elbow as he kissed her on the cheek.

Good morning father, he said to Florian.

Christophe linked arms with the children and they began to cross the courtyard. When they had reached the others, Christophe looked at Florian and pointed to a spot on the ground. The boy sat immediately. Christophe unhooked his arm from Lea's, pulled Florian to his feet, and spun the boy so that he faced the others. Florian did not resist. Then Christophe placed Lea so that she stood perpendicular to the boy, facing the old man. The other children stole sideways glances. They were confused. This was a game none of them had played before, and they did not want to play it wrong.

Isabela kept pulling her hair to her nose and smelling it. Her dress was grass-stained and torn and its hem was muddy. She had walked through the trees to get to the pavilion. Now she looked at Christophe with feigned bewilderment. She had not brought her vows, nor greeted any of the guests, nor even spoken to her uncle. Christophe thought it best to start the ceremony immediately.

The old man closed his eyes and whispered.

We are gathered here today in the face of this company, to join together Christophe and Isabela in matrimony. They will no longer be two, but one flesh. The lord is compassionate to all his creatures. What god has united, man must not separate.

Christophe stood with his mouth agape and trembling as he struggled to remember his next words. His brow knitted with effort and his hands closed into fists. The children stared. Lea put her thumb into her mouth and began sucking it. Florian did not move. Suddenly Christophe's face beamed with uncontained joy and he loosened his fists and opened his eyes, gazing at the open sky, the sun causing him to squint, and the old man remained that way for a few moments before turning his face to the gathered children. It took on a shadowy aspect as he inspected each of their faces.

The priest was faltering. Nobody could be counted on. Only oneself. Christophe turned to Isabela and began his vows.

I, Christophe Guillot, take you, Isabela Jakab, to be my wife. I promise to be true to you in good times and in bad, in sickness and in health. I will love you and honor you all the days of my life.

Christophe's face was very close to Lea's. She could see herself reflected in his pupils, a small figure in the milky veil of age. The courtyard receded and the old man's face came into sharp focus. New details appeared there. Lea saw brown liver spots folded into the creases of his greyish skin. Only his cheeks were smooth and turning a pale pink from excitement. Where his wild grey hair did not grow, down the center of his pate, plaques of dead skin peeled away. Lea looked down at the old man's hands. He held them towards her at hip level, wrists limp and fingers bent at the knuckles. They were covered in the same liver stains as his face. She had never noticed these brown marks before. They were like forest moss appearing overnight on the fresh deadfall. Veins were visible beneath the skin of Christophe's forearms, knotting in places, with a burl where they crossed the wrist, tributaries of thicker vessels that ran alongside and crossed over the four metacarpals, four girders laid from wrist to knuckle.

Lea placed her hands atop Christophe's. She felt there the worn landscape of his life and toil. The veins were soft and they displaced beneath her fingers. There was no excess flesh in the old man's sinewy hands. Lea's were plump and delicate in comparison. Her fingernails were long and their tips were filthy, but her flesh shone a healthy pink. A warm drop of rain fell onto Lea's left hand. When she looked up, she saw that it was not rain. The old man was crying. Drops were gathering at his chin and falling onto their hands.

When it came time for Isabela to say her vows Christophe began weeping. It was the first time she had seen him cry. He did so because he knew he had betrayed her trust by reading her notebook. After wrapping her body in a tarp he left it in the living room and began gathering supplies for his journey. Leave the city. This thought repeated in his mind so that it became the backdrop for his actions. Clothes: waterproof k-way, wool hat, wool socks, trench coat, boots, all underwear, all socks, under-shirts, no suits no shirts no need, two sweaters, one to wear while he washed the other, three pairs of pants, nothing sheer, ski coat, never worn to ski, flashlight, spare 4.5 volt battery, camping backpack, dust falling from the closet into his open mouth, stinging his eyes, shaking the bag off, packing the clothes inside, discman, extra double-A batteries, two compact discs, better than leaving it for them, why did they leave any of this, maybe they took the food, they do not care about your clothes or flashlight or discman, all your equipment is ancient, aluminum mess kit, six bottles of water from the pantry, locked pantry, they were in a hurry, swiss army knife, one fork, one spoon, two dishrags, one sponge, her caved-in skull, leave the dish soap, only need water, spaghetti, rice, chickpeas, lentils, crackers, in the canvas bags with anything you can drop at the first sign of danger if on foot, leave the salt and pepper, leisure, excess, waste, frivolity, tooth-brush, toothpaste, soap, her razor sitting on the side of the bathtub, notebook splayed open on the floor, he had seen this notebook before, sitting on the side of the bathtub and leaning down to pick up the notebook, the last page she wrote before they pulled her out of the bathtub still full of water, which is why she was naked when he found her. Notes she was taking for an essay he was not aware of: Structural violence is rarely visible in the present. It inhabits the past or the future. Laws passed or soon to pass, displacements processed or scheduled to be processed. Disease is the same way. It is not violence apparent. It is the dead or slowly dying, the fears of future contamination. Looking back over this century it will become clear to us that the forces governing our world were of this nature.

Putting down the notebook, watching it slip into the water, the pages going dark, the ink spreading over the paper, his razor, his shaving cream, scissors, first-aid kit with everything inside, backpack on his back, the rest in the canvas bag. Christophe carried all the supplies down the stairs with the emergency lights guiding him through the red hush, until he reached -1 and found the car and cursed because he had forgotten the key. He left the backpack leaning against the car and the canvas bag beside it and walked back up the stairs and found the keys and carried Isabela down the stairs slowly, one arm beneath her knees and the other supporting her back, careful not to hit the guardrails, a human shape, a tarp wrapped in rope, until he reached -1 again, difficult to open doors with the body, then kneeling to rest the body on one knee and opening the trunk and laying the body gently down and reaching over the body for the red plastic jerrycan, which he placed in the backseat with the backpack and the canvas bag. He drove to the peripherique, not stopping for red lights but careful to check for other cars, and doing 60 to conserve gas.

The old man was quiet for a long time and the children sat watching him weep, and Lea did not let go of his hands. Christophe then closed his eyes and began whispering again.

I, Isabela Jakab, take you, Christophe Guillot, to be my husband. I promise to be true to you in good times and in bad, in sickness and in health. I will love you and honor you all the days of my life.

The priest now spoke. He pronounced each word solemnly.

Christophe Guillot, do you take Isabela Jakab to be your wife?

Do you promise to be true to her in good times and in bad, in sickness and in health, to love her and honor her all the days of your life?

I do, said the old man.

Isabela Jakab, do you take Christophe Guillot to be your husband? Do you promise to be true to him in good times and in bad, in sickness and in health, to love him and honor him all the days of your life?

Lea said nothing. Her feet squirmed together.

I do, whispered Christophe. He opened his eyes. He slipped one hand from beneath Lea's and searched in one pant pocket, then the other. His eyes went wide and his face drained of emotion.

I do not have the ring, he said.

Christophe turned to Florian.

Father, he said.

The boy, whose eyes had been downcast, looked up at the old man.

Do you have it? said Christophe.

Florian licked his teeth and said nothing.

I must have let it fall, said Christophe.

The old man dropped to his knees and scuffed his palms in the dust, which raised swirling around him. He coughed and crawled away from the children, stopping to inspect a stone between his grey fingers, then throwing it aside.

This place is dirty, he said to himself.

Christophe picked up another stone. He held it very close to his face, so that his eyes converged and made him look ridiculous. After a long moment he threw it aside. The children sat, watching the old man in silence. A few of them shifted around as they grew increasingly distressed.

The owner does not honor his professional agreements, said the old man as he shook his head.

The trill of birds and the skittering of pebbles echoed in the courtyard. Lea smelled her hair. Florian scratched himself, his eyes darting about the courtyard. Marc glared at the old man.

Will none of you help me find this ring? Christophe said.

The children did not move. He glared at them angrily.

Help me find this fucking ring, Christophe said.

The children were scared. They did not understand what the old man wanted, but scattered across the courtyard and set about imitating him, some running their hands through the dirt, some plucking stray grass, others collecting stones, which they stored in their pockets. All the while they kept an eye on the old man who seemed to despair more with each passing moment. His eyes revulsed and dark patches of sweat spread beneath his arms and in the crook of his back. Dust covered his hands and knees. He pounded the ground with his fist, raising more dust. Rodolphe did the same until the knuckles of his right hand were as bloody as Christophe's and both their wounds were caked with dirt.

It was scratched out in the crimson dirt that Rodolphe saw the path he must take. He would leave the farmhouse with the other children and never return. He would go to a place where neither Christophe nor Marc existed, a place where he could find a strength of his own.

Lucien and Joseph had taken three quarters of an hour to hobble from their home to the top of the farmhouse path. They were old and their bones ached and their joints creaked and they did not hurry. Several times they stopped altogether and used their handkerchiefs to mop their brows and blow their noses. Once they had reached a good vantage point, the old men stopped and observed the courtyard. Human shapes swarmed there like hens pecking at the dirt. Two stood out: a girl wearing a white dress, shabby and soiled, and the larger shape of Christophe in tones of grey and white, no cleaner than the girl. Shoeless, the old man cut a pathetic and twisted figure as he scrabbled about in the dirt. Neither Lucien nor Joseph said anything, nor did their leathery faces move. They had long ago ceased to wear expressions, having become accustomed to the solitude of each other's presence. In one hand Joseph held a plastic bag containing half a dozen eggs. For a long time they observed the scene. Then they turned back.

20.

In the corner of the room, where the shadows gathered, the old man undressed slowly. Lea observed the dark hair between his legs as he bent over to pull his underwear off, lifting one leg, staggering to regain balance, and placing one hand against the wall to avoid falling. His body was orange in the dusk light, skin flaccid beneath his jutting shoulder blades, spine like a rope curving leftwards down the center, each rib delineated by shadow. The old man was smiling when he turned towards her. His eyes no longer frightened Lea. They glowed empty and pure behind the black creases of his face. These were not the eyes of an all-watching being. The old man could not even see what was right in front of him. He stared right through Lea as if she were made of glass. She could no longer afford to fall from her bicycle because he would not be there to pick her up. She felt a tightness behind her jaw where the tears refused to come.

A thin band of filth marked the waistline of the old man's underwear. Lea watched the orange squares of the windowpanes slipping quietly up Christophe's naked body as he approached, becoming more brilliant before they disappeared above his head into the darkening ether. He crouched and slipped into the permanent shadow of the bed, where the old man lay beside the child and looked upon her with vacant adoration. Lea sat cross-legged, picking at her toenails, holding the grime to her nose, that acrid and familiar smell, and finally pulling her hair in front of her face so she would not have to see the old man, who looked pitiful lying there naked on his side, elbow bent on the mattress and head propped in his open palm.

Isabela was drunk but so was he. Too much champagne with dinner, and champagne after dinner, and that sickly-sweet prune digestif Monsieur Chen had insisted they drink. It had put everyone in a good mood, so that even Chen's wife seemed to loosen up and enjoy herself a little. And they had found the ring somehow and finished their vows and kissed. Afterwards most of the guests called taxis, even though they lived nearby, except of course for Isabela's uncle who insisted on driving. But now Isabela was drunk. He knew this because she swayed slightly as she sat on the corner of the mattress, against the wall, still wearing the filthy white gown, hair disarranged, and ordered him to undress. He did so in the corner of the room and lay on the bed beside her and watched her, not wanting the moment to end, so terribly did he feel the ache of love in that moment. He knew he would die without putting words to the feeling. It excluded all else.

Lea watched the old man's eyes glance down to his unmoving prick, hanging limp and larval from his body. She watched his eyes squint and his brow knit and his cheeks lift so that his upper teeth became visible. He looked at Lea and back to his prick. She watched his face become more pallid and sunken. He began sweating. Then with his right hand he reached down and pulled his prick from side to side. After a few moments he withdrew his hand and looked at Lea.

I am sorry my darling, he said. It must be all the champagne.

Lea did not answer. She wished to be upstairs in her bed, not far from Florian, luxuriating in his sleeping presence, and pressed to the cold side of her pillow until it came time to flip it. She wished the old man would return to his former self and cook for them, tend to the garden and wash them, even beat them when it was fair. Lea did not understand why he would choose to become this new thing.

No, said Christophe. Of course not. You are beautiful. You know you are. But there is nothing I can do about it.

The old man closed his eyes and began to snore. Lea watched the flesh of his face and neck tremble and his arm tremble, until it no longer followed the rhythm of his breathing and his wrist loosened and Christophe's head slipped onto the bed, causing him to wake. He looked off into the distance and smiled, his face relaxed and blissful in the dim light. Lea smiled also.

21.

The tomato was rotten. There were blue and white growths on its thin underbelly which split open as Marc lifted it, letting fall a red pulp. The boy dropped the tomato and shook his hands and wiped the transparent pink liquid on the knees of his jumpsuit. The vines were bare and the ground was littered with rotting fruit. Sabine stood squinting in the sunlight as she looked up into an apple tree. She picked an apple from the branch and turned it over in her hands, seeking the wormhole. There was none. Still she did not trust it. She walked over to Marc who was squatting over a rotten lettuce. His smell was buried beneath the general stench of decay. The boy was startled when she tapped his shoulder. His body had become thin and he looked exhausted.

The noises had been keeping all of the children up, the hollow moans coming from the old man's bedroom and lasting through the night. They were muffled by the floor, but still none of them were able to sleep. They had been eating infrequently, as infrequently as the old man's bouts of lucidity.

Sabine gave Marc the apple. He turned it over in his hand. No wormhole. His sister's face was unmoved. He bit the apple and it tasted sweet. Marc took a second bite and handed it to Sabine. She took shallow bites until the skin was gone, and the apple was only a bloated white core. Then she threw it into the grass. Marc picked it up, wiped it on the breast of his jumpsuit, and ate the rest of the flesh. Sabine was squatting over an uneven row of stalks protruding from the dirt. Some were bright green, long with small filaments, and others were a darker green with purple-red streaks on their oblong leaves. Sabine took hold of one of the longer stalks and pulled upwards. The strangled sound of snapping roots could be heard inside the soil as the carrot slid from the earth and Sabine's eyes widened as she fixed upon the orange tuber with clumps of dirt still pressed to it, through which thin orange tendrils reached. Marc walked over to his sister and wrapped his hand around the stalks of several beets. Some snapped, but most unearthed the short round tubers from which they had sprouted. Sabine had already pulled out another carrot and she stood holding both in her outstretched hands, looking at Marc. He thought he could see a smile behind the pallid mask she wore. He laid the beets next to the carrots in her arms and continued pulling tubers. She stood watching him, enjoying the sound they made. He placed each of the beets and carrots in her arms. Soon a pile had amassed. Here had been the food all along, hidden beneath the soil in the place they feared the most. They would feed their children at last, and everything would resume due order. Of course the wild child and the stupid girl would not join them at the dinner table. They would have to find their sustenance elsewhere.

Marc's stomach was empty but his head was filled with a painful clatter of thoughts. His sister wandered towards the farmhouse, arms full of their bounty. That is when Marc noticed the old man framed in the bathroom window as he fixed on Sabine. Marc crouched and watched the scene unfold. His sister stumbling slightly as she made her way towards the path. The old man opening the door, the sound causing Sabine to swing around, eyes uncomprehending, a carrot falling from her arms, and then the rest of what she carried tumbling to the ground, and the old man upon her.

What did I tell you about the garden, he screamed. What did I tell you.

The old man held Sabine by the ankle and reached for a handful of beets. Holding them by the stalks, he swung repeatedly at her wriggling body, rapping her belly and breasts and arms, some of the beets smashing to bits where they struck bone, and the old man finally focusing on the face of the rule-breakers, the niggers and the arabs with their tongues pressed to the floor and searching under the locked door, the men who came, the ones who stole from the store, the sharks buying up the land, the causers of the great sweep, the furious disorder he would never control and from which he could never protect her, and all of his powerlessness in its ugly face, until Sabine's nose had been broken and her face bruised terribly and she had stopped struggling as Marc looked from his crouched position in the dirt and Sabine squealed like a rusted hinge being moved slightly with every blow, not even raising her hands to protect herself.

When Christophe was finished he staggered towards the farmhouse and sat pressed to the wall, in the grass, catching his breath, eyes jittering wildly and muttering unformed words. Marc stayed pressed to the ground among the remaining stalks, saw the old man sweating and rasping and still clutching beets now covered in blood and dirt, the unpredictable animal. He would never underestimate him again. He was more dangerous than before.

Sabine did not move. Nose clogged with blood she elected to breathe through her open mouth instead. Once it filled with blood, she pursed her lips and let the crimson liquid ooze from the sides of her mouth and onto the lobes of her ear and down her neck and into her hair and onto the grass. Her pain was like a disparate constellation of stars strewn across the great black sky. A lot of airless space. Marc stayed pressed to the ground also, and eventually he did not even look but only smelled the dirt and the crushed grass and lay there with his fear among the weeds.

There was the first body in the street, thought the old man. It was a chinese body with a face like a skinned tomato, lying on its back and drawing attention because a chinese woman was chicken-dancing around it, unwilling to touch, but looking at the disappeared face before she resumed her screaming and circling. The body and its family, which they found crammed in a tiny apartment, dead also, were the first of many bodies. I drove Isabela's body south, keeping off the nationales when possible, small roads when possible, and mostly at night. It was before things got too bad anyways. Many people still maintained hope that everything would return to normal. But I knew better. I had seen the hole where Isabela used to smile. Fire hides everywhere. I drove down into the Berri through the sleeping towns, looking for a place that might do. I found the ancient farmhouse with the date still painted on the vertical beam supporting the roof. 1919. Mud and wood and red shingles and nobody around. The farmer probably bought the place with the surrounding fields and never bothered to make any use of it. Left the antiquated equipment right where it stood, focused on revenue instead. No excess resources in agriculture. Perhaps the family with the goat farm. Perhaps the larger-scale operation to the north. After I buried Isabela in the middle of the courtyard, beneath the grass so that it might cover her resting place, a very long time passed before I bothered investigating the area. I ate apples and gooseberries until I was ill. I ate whatever I could find nearby. I withered to nothing. I was a body with no use for a body.

It remained that way for months. Only when the green sapling first protruded from the earth at the center of the courtyard, from Isabela's fallow womb, did my body resume function. From it children and vegetables grew. I have protected both. I have smashed the face of the offender to protect these creatures. Some of us are born liquid. Some of us are born vegetables in the moist earth. We cannot change the sap-thirsty mouth of god with its blue-ocean gums and cliff-sharp teeth. It spits blood from Sabine's mouth onto the grass to be taken back by the earth. Having harmed the child, I sit against the farmhouse, thought the old man, unable to move my body. This part exists disconnected from the body. Having harmed the child.

After hours of waiting and watching the old man, who remained unmoving and expressionless, Marc began crawling towards Sabine. He kept an eye on Christophe, and every time the old man blinked, Marc would stop for a moment to scrutinize his catatonic face.

Sabine was no longer crying when Marc crawled up to her. Her eyes were bloodshot and Marc could see two teeth in the grass, the blood spilling less profusely now, and Sabine no longer spitting as frequently. She breathed through her mouth. Already the swelling had begun around her eyes. The sockets were purple and red where the vessels had burst. Marc helped her stand. They staggered towards the farmhouse, leaving the vegetables broken and scattered, and the old man sitting against the wall. Marc led Sabine through the bathroom. He sat her on a chair in the dining room, standing for a moment to make sure she would not slump and fall. Then he went back into the bathroom and retrieved a towel, which he used to wipe the blood from her face. When he was done she reached for the towel and pressed it to her face and blew blood from her nostrils in one long snort, wiped her nose with the towel, and handed it back to Marc. A strand of blood still hung from one of her nostrils. Marc tried to wipe it away but she would not let him. She would not make eye contact with her brother either. She was a closed chamber of blood, filling with blood, pouring blood, blood in the face and blood in the mouth, missing two teeth, and smelling nothing. Sight narrowing from the swelling. Marc looked at her for a time. Then he walked down the stairs into the kitchen and retrieved a glass from the counter. He filled it with water from the sink, which he could now reach quite easily, and brought it back to Sabine. She did not look at him, but drank from the glass. When she had emptied it her fingers loosened and the glass fell to the ground and shattered on the tile. Glass skittered across the room in all directions. Marc walked back into the kitchen and retrieved the dustpan. He used it to sweep up the glass as he had seen the old man do. Then, not knowing what to do with the glass-filled dustpan, he left it where he had found it beneath the sink. Marc returned to the dining room and sat on a chair near Sabine and watched her until the sun made the room turn gold and red and finally blue with only the moonlight pouring subtly through the window.

He could not hear the other children in the farmhouse or the courtyard or anywhere near. Perhaps they would not return that night. This had become a frequent occurrence. There was no rule of law. The world seethed from no particular central point, and it was for Marc to find his bearing within it. I have done a bad thing, thought Marc.

22.

When Lea and Florian returned to the farmhouse at dawn, they found the old man propped against the wall in the selfsame position. Dew had accumulated on his clothes and skin and his grey face had lost any vestige of color. The children looked at the broken vegetables scattered in the grass around him and the blood. They did not touch them but stood looking at the old man instead. Florian waved his hand in front of Christophe's glazed eyes. No reaction. Florian looked at Lea, who only reflected his own confusion. She leaned down and pulled Christophe's hand, which was cold and hard. The old man rose to his feet, but his eyes did not change. Florian took a few steps back but Lea did not loosen her grip on Christophe's hand. The boy took the old man's other hand and the children led him into the farmhouse, finding the bottom floor empty. The smaller children had not returned to the farmhouse for several weeks now. Perhaps they would never return.

Florian and Lea helped Christophe down the stairs to the kitchen, where they installed him in his rocking chair and sat near him on the torn sofa. They warmed each other with their hands until the last traces of that cold night were gone. Then they curled up in each other's arms and fell asleep, the old man keeping a statue's vigil over the two children as the sun rose steadily over the courtyard.

23.

At first the fire would not come. For a long time Florian stood there in the kitchen, alternately watching the old man and the girl, him sitting very still in his rocking chair, her pawing at the stovetop as it clicked and hissed and emitted strange smells. Then came the fire. The girl knew how to make it appear from where it hid in the kitchen, and for this Florian thought her a god.

Over the next few days, Florian watched the girl feed the old man. She would cut up vegetables made warm by the fire and feed this mush to the grey thing Christophe had become. When these feedings ended, Florian would continue to stare at the old man, who came to act both as an object of fascination and a container for whatever thoughts and feelings were passing through the boy.

The old man's hands now lay resting grey and still in Christophe's lap, denying the great pain they had once caused Florian. His hands no longer protected the garden either, yet it continued to produce food in its messy way under Lea's stewardship. This was good. To Florian, the girl's face was made of the diamond-light and around it swirled the blackness defining every important thing.

The twins were present during this period and Lea systematically shared food with them. Over the weeks Sabine healed slowly without speaking a word. She refused to make eye contact with any of the other children. Marc could always be found near her, observing his sister sheepishly and making sure she ate and drank as needed. His presence disturbed Florian at first. Over time the boy came to accept that Marc no longer seemed animated by fits of violence, but he remained on his guard nonetheless. After a few weeks, Florian felt comfortable enough to wander out into the wilderness and hunt for the group.

24.

The boy moved through the forest slowly and deliberately. His hearing had grown very fine and Florian could hear the dry rasp of his palms against tree trunks, the rabbits twitching in the dryleaf, the birds pattering about, and the wild boar panting through their yellowed tusks. In each of these animals coursed the blood which stove-boiled would yield food for Lea. In their eyes hung the fluid of all light, of all that could be seen, so that in each gelatinous ball the whole world manifested independently, to be extinguished when Florian, having sunk his teeth into their necks, hung there stubbornly until the animals ceased to breathe. Florian, ender of worlds, provider of death, and survivor of the great sweep, in this way moved through the forest until he spotted quarry. And there it was among the moss, the wet quivering of life, a rabbit bristling with the flawed awareness afforded the hunted. Florian waited before lunging. The smaller throats collapsed easily, and the boy did not have to rend the beast for long before it gave up struggling and expired with a gurgle.

Lea stood in the garden collecting apples from the tree, each fruit pulling at the branches before it gave way. The snapping of the apple stem felt agreeable to her. She looked up through the spidering branches at the fruit she might have to climb for, and stopped mid-reach to examine her immaculate fingers caught in the sunlight, the nails having been chewed to perfection, the flesh suckled until it was rosy and clean. Florian liked his nails long. Over time the two had settled on a nighttime tongue-cleaning combined with the use of a knife or twig to scour beneath them. For a time she had simply waited for Florian to fall asleep before chewing his nails, but this always resulted in punishingly long absences on the part of the boy, and so Lea ceased insisting and accepted his desire to wear them long. It was only weeks later that she noticed the blood caked beneath them and understood their usefulness in his daily hunts.

Now that her loneliness existed only as a phantom, Lea spent much of her time planning for the incoming cold. The summer had given way to a temperate autumn but she knew that the old man—sat catatonic with palms open in capitulation—would be of no help. The soil would harden and the vegetables would die and the pantry was not stocked with the usual non-perishables. Christophe had failed to instruct any of the children how to gather these goods from nearby towns. This fact among others caused Lea to realize how little the old man had prepared for his own end.

25.

Sabine watched Christophe bare his teeth, black now, as he began reacting to the knife. The old man's pants lay around him in tatters, cut into uneven ribbons before the girl applied the blade to his inner thighs, where a thin sliver of blood formed in the wake of the blade cutting in long sloping strokes. Otherwise the old man did not move, but merely bled from the legs that had once carried him through the world, throat emitting a soft hiss, not unlike that of a coffee pot in the wane of a boil. Sabine looked at her work as the knife swung again in a red line, many slashes now, birds across the flesh of the sky, with a mechanized logic beyond understanding. She listened to the faint sound of the old man's parting flesh as she pushed the knife deeper, wounds like grey gills running over anemic muscle from which blood poured in a curtain, mixing with the air as it struck the ground and shifted from red to black. The valley was a red valley, and it bled with the same dispassion as a brook babbles and a river flows and an ocean stirs and the black blood of stars pools dully between them, those bright punctures to which we crane our necks in wonder. Sabine cradled each testicle briefly before she sliced through the scrotum, severing the cremaster muscle and the spermatic cord, arteries, blood spraying now, from the old man's groin and onto the kitchen tile. His eyes fluttered and his chin raised and the nape of his neck lifted from the rocking chair.

Christophe stared longingly at the ceiling of the farmhouse, the beams, the white between them, the light of his last day wobbling through the familiar windows, a painful breath of color, the searing spectrum of what is felt, and the rot of actuality creeping like frost across a puddle. The blue is being taken from the sky, thought Christophe. Soon there will be nothing to raise my hands to. He squinted at the sun looming white above the playground. It was expanding. He could smell the fat green birdshit. It was everywhere in the dirt, on the green benches, on the swing set even. He could hear the splattering too. The pigeons were sick from the green fruit of spring, dropping oily shits from the branches of the chestnut trees. Even the supervisors were worried for their trench coats.

I warn you, Christophe. No future was built without hands. Idle time is a luxury even children cannot afford. But the sun came to take the blue anyway, thought Christophe. So maybe they were wrong after all.

The old man was dead by the time Lea entered the dining room. He sat drained of malice in the armchair, Sabine on all fours at his feet, her white palms pressed to the kitchen floor, fingers lost in a thick layer of stagnant blood, the legs of her jumpsuit black and blackening as the cloth slowly sucked the liquid upwards. Lea dropped the apples and they tumbled across the dining room tile. She bounded down the stairs and into the kitchen where her shoe struck the back of Sabine's head, Sabine not resisting but instead exploring this new suffocation with curiosity, eager to discover what lay behind this final curtain of suffering, her skull with each kick crushed further along that path, through the old man's blood and through the kitchen floor and into the dancing lights of the afterworld where no part of her soul had been extinguished.

When Sabine ceased her twitching, Lea hoisted herself into the armchair and sat on Christophe's lap. She squeezed his hard face between her fingers, kissed his cold forehead, and wept. A series of agonized sounds could be heard echoing through the structure. Creaking, shifting, the petrified muscles threatened collapse. Through her tears Lea stared at the shoulder beams slumping beneath the heavy ceiling. Drained of flesh and bone, the mummified pillars could no longer hold the weight of the celestial spheres.

The great sweep was over. But tomorrow had not yet begun.

26.

Marc stood in the dining room and stared at his sister's upended body, blonde hair spreading like sunlight through the pearled crimson, shoe marks in the uncombed strands, jumpsuit soaked in blood. He saw the corpse of the old man in the rocking chair with its legs like pale rods from which red drapes hung. Something was moving in its lap. The girl. Her eyes were bloodshot with grief as she looked up, hopeful at first that it might be the wild boy, then fearful as she saw it was Marc, her brown eyes and snot-caked mouth agape, the little murderous rat.

Marc slipped as he sprinted down the steps, twisting as he fell and slid through the dark liquid. By the time he was back on his feet Lea had already leapt up the steps and across the living room, fumbling with the door handle until she burst into the cold sunlight of the courtyard. Once she had reached the edge of the field she looked back at the farmhouse to see the red and furious face of the huntsman crossing its threshold. There was nothing to do but run.

The fields were yellow and green. The fields were yellow. The fields were dry in the summer. The fields were sparse and incomplete. Weeds grew between the meager stalks. The stalks parted for the gasping child as it ran towards the forest.

Lea caught sight of Florian as Marc overtook her. A lone shape emerging from the treeline, the boy's mouth bloody as he cradled a sleeping rabbit in his long white fingers.

Note to Reader

Thank you for reading *Fire Hides Everywhere*. I have written two other books: *Even the Red Heron* (2014), *And We Came to Find It Beautiful* (2015). You can find both on Amazon. For more news about my work, both literary and otherwise, you can find me at julianfeeld.com, on Facebook going by FEELD, or on Twitter as julianfeeld.

Sincerely,

Julian

Recent bestsellers from Zero Books are:

In the Dust of This Planet
Horror of Philosophy vol. 1
Eugene Thacker
In the first of a series of three books on the Horror of
Philosophy, *In the Dust of This Planet* offers the genre of horror
as a way of thinking about the unthinkable.
Paperback: 978-1-84694-676-9 ebook: 978-1-78099-010-1

Capitalist Realism
Is there no alternative?
Mark Fisher
An analysis of the ways in which capitalism has presented itself
as the only realistic political-economic system.
Paperback: 978-1-84694-317-1 ebook: 978-1-78099-734-6

Rebel Rebel
Chris O'Leary
David Bowie: every single song. Everything you want to know,
everything you didn't know.
Paperback: 978-1-78099-244-0 ebook: 978-1-78099-713-1

Cartographies of the Absolute
Alberto Toscano, Jeff Kinkle
An aesthetics of the economy for the twenty-first century.
Paperback: 978-1-78099-275-4 ebook: 978-1-78279-973-3

Malign Velocities
Accelerationism and Capitalism
Benjamin Noys
Long listed for the Bread and Roses Prize 2015, *Malign Velocities*
argues against the need for speed, tracking acceleration as the
symptom of the on-going crises of capitalism.
Paperback: 978-1-78279-300-7 ebook: 978-1-78279-299-4

Meat Market
Female flesh under Capitalism
Laurie Penny
A feminist dissection of women's bodies as the fleshy fulcrum of
capitalist cannibalism, whereby women are both consumers and
consumed.
Paperback: 978-1-84694-521-2 ebook: 978-1-84694-782-7

Poor but Sexy
Culture Clashes in Europe East and West
Agata Pyzik
How the East stayed East and the West stayed West.
Paperback: 978-1-78099-394-2 ebook: 978-1-78099-395-9

Romeo and Juliet in Palestine
Teaching Under Occupation
Tom Sperlinger
Life in the West Bank, the nature of pedagogy and the role of a
university under occupation.
Paperback: 978-1-78279-637-4 ebook: 978-1-78279-636-7

Sweetening the Pill
or How we Got Hooked on Hormonal Birth Control
Holly Grigg-Spall
Has contraception liberated or oppressed women? *Sweetening
the Pill* breaks the silence on the dark side of hormonal
contraception.
Paperback: 978-1-78099-607-3 ebook: 978-1-78099-608-0

Why Are We The Good Guys?
Reclaiming your Mind from the Delusions of Propaganda
David Cromwell
A provocative challenge to the standard ideology that Western
power is a benevolent force in the world.
Paperback: 978-1-78099-365-2 ebook: 978-1-78099-366-9